EXTINCTION ISLAND 2
FEAR THE EYES

catt dahman

ISBN 978-1-925225-98-3

Chapter 1: Nests

The nest was wide, built of leaves, sticks, and feces-caked mud, and raked into place by the adults: twenty-foot long dinosaurs called ceratosaurus. Mashed into the muck of the nest and adding to the stench were bits of dropped fish and flesh from recent kills.

Babies chirped, birdlike, and gulped pieces of the rotten meat. Colored a soft, peachy brown, the ceratosaurus had pebbled skin, and frequently broke or rubbed away bristled feathery hairs along their spines when they scratched their backs on trees. They were like birds and crocodiles, displaying traits of both creatures, remnants of feathers and scales.

Carrying food in her mouth, a female adult paused and snorted as she returned to the nest where her eggs had recently had hatched. Pieces of the pale peach eggshells broke under her weight since she weighed almost a full ton.

Procreation and strength as a hunting pack were of utmost concern. She was responsible for protecting the little ones and teaching them skills. Teaching methods were based on punishment, never reward, because they didn't understand the concept.

The other juveniles and smaller babies gathered around the female adult who set her haul into the bottom of the nest. She lowered her head and snapped the head off the man she had put in the nest. She crunched a few times and then swallowed.

The adults had already eaten, so what was left, was for the little ones. Most of the cloth was already torn away from the *food*; the waistband and half a leg of denim were matted with mud and stained green from vegetation.

Hardly using its powerful jaws and blade-like teeth, one of the babies grabbed fingers and gulped them. The gold band on the ring finger vanished into the baby's maw. Then, the baby immediately tore a chunk from the swollen, blackened flesh of an arm.

One of the babies rolled over the lip of the nest as he played with the other babies, and the female adult stepped on its leg, causing it to shriek.

Each of the baby's hind legs was muscular and strong, but the female adult mashed his leg against a rock that was barely covered by a thin film of mud and green ooze. Because his lower leg and one toe were broken, the pain caused him to limp around and squeal.

The mother of the injured juvenile ceratosaurus leaned down and sniffed the baby. Using her big nose and head, she rolled the baby over several times, trying to force it to get up and stand. She rolled her big yellow eyes as she looked at the baby.

Despite the pain, the small dinosaur rose on his back legs, waving its small but powerful forelegs in the air and squeaking. Like his parents, the baby had ridges over his eyes, a small nasal horn, and raised osteodermal platelets from head to tail like those of a crocodile. The platelets had protected his spine and saved him from instant death.

The baby was not only emitting cries of pain, which might alert a larger predator, but it also showed a weakness in the pack. The cries disturbed the other snorting members who were blowing dust and moisture from large nasal cavities and frightening birds and small animals.

The mother nudged the baby, pushing him farther from the nest and closer to the forest. She worked until he stopped fighting and lay against a rotting log, panting and terrified. She walked away, leaving him to die among the debris.

After he died, whether in a few hours or a full day, he would become food for the pack, a small morsel that would have no connection to the others of his kind.

Usually the adults brought back the common fare: lizards, birds, other dinosaurs, fish, or unfortunate animals from the trees, even some that were furry.

The ceratosaurus were excellent swimmers, able to stretch out to their maximum length and use their enormous tails to propel them across the water's surface. Able to dive as well as they could swim, they were exceptional fishers, just as pleased with rotting fish as with fresh.

While fleeing from a predator, the man had the bad luck to run into the water and drown. It was the good luck of the creatures to find a different kind of tasty meal in the lake.

It was a fluke for humans and dinosaurs to encounter one another, but this was Extinction Island, and the impossible was routine.

Chapter 2: On the Beach

"How are they?"

Kelly frowned at Air Marshal Lynn and shrugged, "I can't tell. They're banged up. We can treat the bumps, cuts, and bruises, but there isn't a lot to do for mental shock and loss."

"I mean, how *are* they mentally?"

"Like anyone else here. Scared. Confused. Suspicious of us," said Kelly as she pushed by him and walked out to stand by the campfire. Her movements weren't of rudeness, but of frustration that any caregiver might feel.

She could treat a cut or a bruise, but injuries that were more serious were beyond her ability, and injuries of the spirit and mind were impossible for her to deal with. She and those with her would deal with reality and move on, or would go insane. It was the reality of the island.

Kelly and her friends had been on a yacht, enjoying a private cruise, and were enamored with the beautiful scenery and the warm waters to swim in. Those same waves became like battering rams as the wind blew in a storm and blasted them, tossing them around the cabins like dolls.

The crash onto the island seemed like an abrupt, but good ending to the barrage of winds and waves, but the real nightmares began after they landed.

Her new patients were nestled in the ruins of the huge yacht, home to the survivors, and protected from the elements or things even worse. It was where some mended, if healing were an option. Kelly was able to clean up those who recently crashed, soothe their cuts and scratches, and nod as they wept.

"I don't understand," John Littleton, captain of the *Violet Marie,* said for at least the tenth time. He was scraped and bruised, and most of his crew and friends were lost to the sea. Only his best friend's wife and two teenagers had survived the violent storm that tossed his boat onto the island and swallowed everyone else.

He was still in shock from the violence of the storm, his own injuries, and his losses. He kept repeating himself and looking at each person for some answers.

Helen brushed her dark hair off her neck and tilted her head with sympathy and said, "I'm sorry. We don't know everything, either, John. We *know* we crashed here after a storm. We *know* your boat crashed here after a storm. We *know* planes and boats that vanished between Florida and Bermuda washed up on the beach. You can see the remains for yourself: planes crashed in the jungle."

"Bermuda Triangle bullshit?" asked Littleton, who wasn't sure if this were a sick joke, or if he didn't understand what was being said. "I don't get why no one has come to help us."

"We *have*. There is no one else except us. We're alone," Helen said.

"Because of this joke? You have to be kidding."

Stu laughed bitterly and said, "I wish. For the first time, I wish I were wrong about everything. In the morning, walk down the beach and see the old remains of the *Violet Marie,* and then walk back to the new remains of your boat. Explain all this to me in a way that doesn't scare the hell out of me." He was angry because the rules were broken. He didn't like how nothing fit into his mind in orderly ways.

Stu had seen and touched the old remains of the *Violet Marie,* which were way down the beach. He wasn't the only one who knew the story, or rather the scary legends of Littleton and the lost boat. It was all part of the Bermuda Triangle lore.

During the last storm, the waves deposited a boat, the *Violet Marie*, on the sand. John Littleton was staring at Stu and arguing possibilities. It might not be *possible,* but it was *real.*

"You're saying my boat is there, and over there? *Both* places? It's some trick, right? A joke?"

"I'm afraid not. We can debate this forever, but the fact is that somehow, your boat is in two places. I'm not an expert with science, but despite everything, it's real. You're here, and Stu and a few of the others heard all about your disappearance five years ago. I know. Impossible."

"I want to know when help is arriving," Littleton told Helen.

Stu banged his palm against his forehead. "There is no help. How can there be help when you have crashed here twice and are in two places at once? Look at my brother. See where Kelly removed his arm? It's a fresh injury. Want to know what happened? Dinosaurs."

John Littleton blinked and chuckled, "This is a joke on me, right?" His eyes were too bright, and his skin was pale. Everyone knew that *he* was aware that deep down, this wasn't a joke and that Littleton was terrified. At the very least, the people he was with must be insane.

Tyrese, the leader of their group, slowly explained again that they had been caught in a storm that came up as a yellow fog and caused enormous waves that tore the yacht apart. Those aboard had suffered broken bones, bruises, and cuts, while others drowned. Using the limited medical supplies she had, Kelly treated the injured, suturing and bandaging for hours.

As they explored the island, looking for fresh water and food, the scouting parties found giant beasts, dinosaurs that never should have existed in this time. Unfortunately, the creatures were hungry and preyed on the survivors. "Think of it as an island with giant beasts," Tyrese said, trying to be helpful.

"Dinosaurs." Littleton shook his head. He let his eyes travel over some of the bare bones lying around camp, and they did look to be of prehistoric size to him. Instead of being fossils, they were fresher.

"It doesn't matter what you think now. You'll see them. It's not as if we can hide them, right?" Stu asked.

"There are far more, but I don't think you'd believe half of it," Helen said. "I'm here, and I still have to pinch myself to stay in reality, but look, you're in a better place than we were. We didn't know anything when we came here. We can explain things to you."

"I just want to get Jada and the kids to a hospital and then see about finding the rest. They might have washed up, and if so, there will be a body recovery."

Stu stared at John Littleton and said, "We did that, too. We waited for help. It isn't coming. I don't even understand how you can be here now. It's a paradox. You have proven Einstein right, or wrong, but I can't decide which."

Kelly sighed and said, "Let's focus on what we know. John, I think your friends will be okay, but Jada is emotionally raw from the loss of her husband. She has a head wound, but I think she will make it. The teenagers are scraped and cut, but are okay."

"What kind of dinosaurs?"

Everyone turned and looked at Benny, one of the survivors who washed up with Littleton. He was twelve and curious. With no self- consciousness, he walked across the sand, limping a little because of the soreness, and he smiled at Joe, the cook, from the original group.

Benny's eyes were expectant and interested, but he also had a kind of maturity to his face that made him seem older. He was the type some would call an *old soul.*

Joe smiled broadly and handed Benny a plate without being asked. Thanks to salvage expeditions into the airplane cargo holds, the survivors had most of the comforts of home, just minus the home. Benny looked at the food by the campfire's light, frowned, and asked, "What's this? It smells good." He didn't sound critical or particular about the food, only interested.

"Some canned beans we salvaged and some vegetation from this place, and the meat of a dinosaur. What kind, Alex?"

"Compsognathus."

"I know about that species," Benny said. He took a bite of the meat, nodded, and said, "It tastes like chicken."

"Benny…" Littleton didn't finish.

Joe laughed. "Yep, it does."

"How did dinosaurs get here?"

"We don't know. There are all kinds," Alex said. "Maybe it's just an island that has animals that didn't go extinct."

"That's not true," Stu said, "because you know there are other things here like the *Violet Marie*."

"I don't think we know enough to tell people they are time traveling or caught in some paradox. We only know there are anomalies," Alex said.

"Predators and prey? Yeah. There is a full eco-system here, I guess. How big is the island? I don't think animals can grow very big here in isolation, and I bet there aren't the big monsters like a T-Rex or triceratops, right? The island can't support that kind of life," said Benny, as he ate more. "Have you seen any of those? The big ones?"

Alex stared. Thus far, he had been the best source they had for dinosaur behavior. He suddenly felt he was less alone with his ponderings. It made sense that a younger person would be interested in dinosaurs. "No. That's been my theory, too. We haven't investigated much, but we do know a few species are large, but again, we just don't know enough to say."

"There are lots of islands that people will never find. I don't see why it's so improbable to have dinosaurs on the island, Alex. As for the rest, I don't know. I have to think about it some more and see how quantum physics could apply," Benny said.

"Are you some crazy genius?" Stu asked Benny.

"I'm not crazy, because my mom had me tested for that. I'm a little socially awkward. I'm also not a genius; again, that was tested, but I am smart," Benny said as he burped, covering his mouth. "We can talk time travel later. Have the dinosaurs attacked you?"

"Yes, several times. That's why we lost a few people after we crashed here, and that is why we have a few people who are wounded. The dinosaurs are aggressive."

"You're easy prey, they think. If you killed enough of them, over time, they would develop genetic memories and avoid humans, I think, but that would take several generations."

Alex was excited, "Exactly." He was happy to have someone who thought as he thought. In all honesty, Benny might be far brighter. The only other person who knew much about the creatures was Sue, and she was listening to Benny as well, fascinated.

Stu scowled and said, "There are cannibals, too. Kids from the plane crash."

Air Marshal Lynn jerked and no longer sat stretched out. He tensed. The kids were from his air flight, so he still took it personally that they went off alone and went feral.

He often thought about the early days of the plane crash, and as the lone lawman, he wondered what he should have done to save more of his friends.

"Really? Why? There must be plenty of food here," Benny said.

"You have to be kidding me," Littleton said. "Are all of you on drugs?"

"Not anymore," Davey said.

Helen shook her head, smothering a grin at Davey. "We were going to tell them a little at a time so that they could adjust and take it all in, right? Way to go, Stu."

"No one went easy on me and told me gently," Stu said.

"Cannibals?" Benny asked, "Really?"

"Sort of. They weren't originally, but they were in a plane crash. When they explored, they found a pool of water that we've since had the chance to explore." Helen didn't want to remember the bad things that happened at the pool of water or how it affected people. "The young people swam there and drank steroid-infused water. The water leeched the steroids out of plants that grew around it. It's natural but concentrated in the water. Some plants…"

"Contain steroids. Yup," Benny finished the statement. He pointed to Alex and nodded, "You figured it out? Brilliant. They are aggressive because of that. The kids, I mean. It makes sense: cannibals, dinosaurs, and the Bermuda Triangle. Wow, things around here sure go big, pun intended." He was interested, just short of being excited.

"We're going to kill the bastards. They slaughtered one of our group," Stu said.

Mattie, one of the women who sat around the fire, made a noise and wrapped her arms around herself. The leader of the feral children was her son.

"Unless you killed Lori," Air Marshal Lynn said. He pointed to Stu.

"We already had this talk. Stu didn't do it," Helen reminded him. "He didn't because we discussed it, and we came to the conclusion that the kids were to blame. That's his mother, Mattie. It's a sensitive subject."

Alex said, "Stu was blamed at first because of some misleading evidence, but when we talked to him and reexamined what was there at the site of the murder, we found proof that Stu was not guilty." He wasn't able to say *innocent*, but it was as close as he could get. Stu had done several things that were not murderous, but they were not exactly *innocent*, either.

"I'm still going to kill them," Stu said.

"Knock it off," Tyrese said, "and let's stand guard duty. Joe, take that woman and girl some food. Kelly, you might want to check on them, and take Benny back and let him rest. It's been stressful. Mr. Littleton, we'll find you a place to rest, and maybe in the morning, everything will begin feeling real. I'm truly sorry you ended up here with us."

Helen nodded and said, "That's best for now. We're all sorry, Mr. Littleton."

"I am, too. Right now, I think all of you are crazy, or maybe I am having a nightmare." Littleton wrapped a protective arm around Benny and decided he needed some time to take in the information and decide what to do. "Bad nightmares."

Helen said, "I wish. At least with nightmares, you wake."

John Littleton was sore, and he went to a pallet to sleep, wondering what kind of insanity he had wandered into. He thought about the group who claimed that they crashed in a yacht; he believed that part. The other few who said they crashed in the jungle with their plane going down in the trees were believable as well.

In the morning, he would go for help.

Alone, he cried for the loss of his friends and crew and felt terribly sorry for himself, as he tried to sleep. He wanted to make a plan to get help for himself, Jada, Amy, Benny, but that would have to be executed in the morning, and his mind twisted and turned as he tried to make sense of everything.

In the distance, he heard strange noises: roars and squeals. The reverberations were so unfamiliar and eerie that his arms broke out in chill bumps. *What kind of creature made those sounds?*

As Littleton started to wonder about everything he had been told, he grew more afraid. Disbelief was far easier; reality was going to terrify him.

Someone in the ruins of the yacht wept, making John Littleton feel less alone, but also more frightened, and it was a long time before he slept.

Chapter 3: Rescue Party

Scott dug his boot into the sand, covered it, and then shook it clean as he tried to restrain his anger. Alex and he had already cursed and demanded answers, but nothing helped their concern. After everything they had been through, how could a group simply walk into the jungle without taking a few who could protect them?

He and a few others had late guard duty and slept later to make up for those hours. While they slept, some of their group made unthinkable mistakes.

"Tyrese went with them," Stu said. "Isn't he the so-called leader, now?" His voice dripped with sarcasm, irritating Scott.

"I told you to go," Tom told his brother. He rubbed the stump of his arm, somehow knowing what his brother would reply.

"You aren't the leader anymore," Stu said. "You were replaced. It's too bad this group doesn't want anyone with brains to lead."

Tom sighed. It was as he expected. From the time they crashed, until recently, he had stepped up as a leader,his friends and attempting to fight anything that threatened them, since he had invited them on the cruise.

After Tom's arm became infected, Kelly removed it, despite his protests. Now, he was no longer seen as a leader; he was the one-armed man who was ignored. It was curious how an infection took his arm, his position, and his worth. "Brains? I only wish."

"Scott, you can't boss everyone in camp. Tyrese is the leader, and he went with the group," said Kelly as she rolled her eyes. She didn't want more drama and derision in the group.

"I'm not saying I'm the boss, but this isn't *right*."

"How many times have all of you been to the spring for water? Why are you so upset?" Kelly asked.

Alex answered for Scott, saying, "First, most of *those* people have never been in the jungle, so they are inexperienced with the shit that's out there. Second, Littleton and Benny just landed here and they are not healthy. They have injuries, and of all people,

Kelly, you should appreciate that. Third, can't you hear the noises?"

Kelly tightened her lips. Alex had a point. Because of the recent rains or because of something else, the animals were far louder than normal: hooting, snorting, roaring, and stamping. She thought Alex was right about all of his points, but she disliked being wrong. "Maybe they got lost or are taking their time."

Alex rolled his eyes. "Those two possibilities are *exactly* why I'm worried. Both are dangerous."

"So is everything else we do right here!" Kelly snapped at him. "We have to be able to gather fresh water, or we will have a huge problem."

Scott said, "We can get water but not until people are better prepared to go into the jungle. We have trouble almost every time we go."

Helen used her fingers to mark off each person's name. "Pam, Sue, Shonna, Littleton, Benny, Tyrese, Durango, and Davey? Eight. Of those, two are prepared. Unreal."

"Sue is maybe the third most dependable. Really, Tyrese and Davey are all they have for protection," Alex agreed.

"I didn't send them," Kelly said, and went to finish her work. She was rubbing oil into Amanda's back, hoping that the burned flesh and deep cuts would loosen so Amanda was no longer forced to arch her back.

Although the healing had gone well and fast at first, it had been too fast, and now, Amanda was suffering. Kelly felt guilt tugging at her and knew that was why she snapped at the others. She was using medical alternatives she didn't understand. She also was the one who cauterized Amanda's back instead of letting her die of the wounds. Nothing was easy.

Sometimes people were angry when Kelly couldn't save them, but other times they were upset over Kelly's methods. No one had given Kelly answers about how to work or who to save. She was a nurse, and at this point, she figured that she was a poor excuse for one.

"They should have been back. I have a bad feeling," Scott said. He watched the line of trees where the jungle ended and the beach began, hoping to see the other group coming back. Since they had landed and found dinosaurs, he protected everyone, learning how to fight with sticks and knives.

Davey, Tyrese, Helen, Alex, and Scott had fought as a team several times and had a sort of routine formed. Without the team, Davey and Tyrese had a disadvantage. Adding Benny's excitement and Littleton's suspension of believability was a definite liability.

"Dad is stronger, but he isn't right. He is weak mentally since hitting his head and receiving the head injury during the storm and then the wreck," Tom said. He worried about his father, Durango.

"Durango has trouble with his vision, too," Scott agreed. "I think we will have to search for them."

"I say we wait," Stu said. He didn't want his younger brother, Vaughn, to go looking in the jungle where there was danger. Tom still didn't venture far, and Stu's mother and sister didn't bother to do much more than complain. If Vaughn wanted to go looking for their father, then Stu had a problem.

"I say we can't wait," said Scott as he glared. Stu and he had fistfights before, but Scott didn't want to fight again because he might not win, but he wasn't going to be bullied either.

He saw the way Stu's eyes looked over to Vaughn and understood the issue. "You, Tom, and Vaughn can hold things down here, right?"

"Sure," Stu said as he narrowed his eyes. It gave him a way to protect his brother.

The island was beautiful with pristine white beaches licked by warm and gentle aqua waves. The lush, plump green foliage and blooming flowers in all colors were abundant in the jungle. It was obscene that the island was inhabited by feral children, dotted with wreckages that were confusing to find, and was populated by dinosaurs. Even the word *dinosaur* felt unreal.

As bad as that was, or as juxtaposed as the elements were, some of the people with Scott made him just as angry. At times, it felt that some of them worked separate agendas or enjoyed being assholes. Kelly was over-worked and emotional, and Tom was angry and injured, but Scott didn't really harbor any anger towards either of them.

Stu was another issue altogether. Even in the face of other evidence or opinions, he was aggressive, insisting he was always correct, but tended to stay out of the action except to cause more problems.

Scott nodded and said, "Then, we're good."

Stu shrugged, "Whatever you think, I'm staying here to protect my sister, mom, and brother."

"I don't need ya, Stu," Tom said.

"I meant my other brother."

"He's okay staying here. I feel better that way," Scott told Tom.

"You don't trust me?" Stu asked.

"I do as far as you trust me," said Scott as he carefully chose his words. Kelly chewed her bottom lip with concern.

Lately, she and Stu, formerly almost enemies, were getting closer. Before the shipwreck, she almost had been engaged to Tom, but now, Tom was close to Joy who had made the rounds of the camp, sleeping with almost every man in the group before she settled down with Tom. The drama was enough to cause Scott's head to ache, and he wished they would draw a diagram of all the changing relationships.

It pissed Scott off to have to worry about the group's dynamics. He asked, "Alex? Sorry, but…"

"I'm with you," Alex agreed. He swallowed a tiny lump of fear. He had always been the smart man, the brainy man, or the studious man, but now, because of circumstances, he had to be a fighter. He was lucky that he learned to swing heavy bats and stab with knives.

When he wasn't fighting for his life, like right now, he was kind of proud that Scott asked him to be his second. He never thought he would be trusted as a protector.

"I know I can depend on you. You think on your feet."

Alex flushed and said, "Thanks, I try."

Scott asked Air Marshal Lynn to remain at camp, mainly because he was the best bet the survivors had if Stu did something stupid, or if anything attacked. Scott had to think three steps ahead.

Lynn seemed to understand, so he winked and said, "I have this under control. Nothing is going to come knocking up close."

Joe laughed, breaking the tension and said, "If it does, I hope the marshal kills it so we can have steaks. Smoking them and eating them sounds good. Kill it, and I'll cook it."

"What about me?" Helen asked. She knew Scott worried about her, but he always trusted her to have his back, literally. She was loyal and in love with Scott, something she discovered on the island. Despite their feelings, she didn't want him to pamper her. She could fight when needed.

Worried about her safety, Scott agreed that Helen should come with them, but was also sure that she was one of the most reliable people on the island. In his view, she was amazing. The priest, Father Robert, or Bobby as they called him, and RJ, finished out the team. They were strong fighters as well.

With knives and sticks, the group looked less than formidable, but they moved quietly and quickly into the tree line, unnerved by the noises. They were a good team.

"Be safe," Kelly called.

"Why is everything so loud?" Scott asked Alex. He jumped each time there was a loud roar or an echoing snuffle. Thrashing and cracking sounded as if a war were being waged.

"I'm not sure. Usually the animals and birds get quiet if something is hunting," said Alex as he thought it over.

"So there might not be a pack hunting here? I hear all the snorts, though," Helen said.

As Alex nodded, he said, "I didn't explain well. I mean if a pack is hunting, ordinarily the rest of the critters get quiet. I'm afraid there is more than one pack running around this morning. That might account for all the noise. Instead of stealthy work, the packs could be clashing. It's all I can think of to explain the noise."

"Why would that happen? Why would several packs be drawn here?" RJ asked.

"Oh, because we've disrupted the eco-system each time we have killed a meat eater or a plant eater. May be the storms, or may be eight people that went blundering into the jungle. May be all of those reasons at once."

Alex pointed. The trail was packed down, and vegetation grew away or was pruned back by the passing of humans and animals.

Sometime, instead of walking in a line, a few people walked together, breaking and mashing the foliage. Leaves were bruised, and branches randomly were broken, causing sap to ooze.

Scott knelt and said, "I see that Tyrese's boot prints are in the center of the trail and that sneaker prints are all over the place. Ty wouldn't have thought about it because we normally walk in a line. They had to make a lot of noise coming through here."

Coming up to the spring of fresh water was the most dangerous, because it was where packs of predators hid in order to ambush plant eaters or smaller meat eaters. Tyrese and Davey knew that, but evidently, the rest didn't listen because the footprints scattered farther, making it clear that some of the group had rushed to the water without watching and listening first.

Scott felt Tyrese must have been pulling his hair out by the time they got this far. He knew Tyrese would have been furious, but it wasn't easy to boss around this group of people.

Enormous, wheezing grunts and snorts filled the jungle. A roar cut away to loud snapping sounds. Scott and his group knew the sounds and what they meant. A large beast was feeding, and the cracking noises were the snapping of bones. Goose bumps formed on their arms.

Alex made a motion, indicating they shouldn't go forward, but needed to wait. It was too dangerous to try to get to the water. He jerked his head to one side where it looked as if someone had gone off the path. He put a finger to his lips.

The canopy of the jungle was not only the top of trees, but it also was comprised of a majority of the foliage: mosses, vines, ferns, and algae that grew twined through the branches of trees. The trees struggled for sunlight, blocking the lower areas that were below the hundred-foot canopy.

As soon as the members of the group saw the tiny clearing, they froze, listening for sounds of a predator and trying to make sense of what they saw.

Many of the ferns were mashed deeply into the ground and were covered by heavy splashes of bright red blood. A man lay on his side, and several seconds passed before they realized the bloated, greenish figure was Durango, his skin beginning to turn greyish black.

Scott felt sick with fear and loss. For years, when he was around Tom and the family, Durango was like another father to him, always supportive and kind. He had been strong and loud, a bigger-than-life personality that changed after his head injury. Scott had not mourned the loss because Durango was still alive, but he was just a different Durango.

"Durango," Helen whispered, "oh, no." She also loved the big, brawny man who took the time to tell her about the ocean and teach her as they sailed. She loved Tom's father. He was like Tom and Vaughn in temperament, but loud like Stu.

Durango didn't move. He was obviously dead, yet, the reason why the scavengers hadn't started eating his flesh was confounding, a confounding question and an unknown. It would have been horrible to see him being eaten. Scott looked at Alex who shrugged and shook his head as they crept forward.

"Stu and Tom are going to lose it," Helen said. They were the only ones with family on the island. Durango had commanded the yacht, and Tom had invited his college friends to go along, but Stu, their mother Connie, his other brother Vaughn, and sister Vera, had been along for the trip, but not around the rest as much as Tom and Durango had been.

Everyone liked Durango. Helen felt hurt and asked, "What happened to him?"

The second body lay close to Durango and was barely recognizable, as Sue, a pretty Asian woman who had not only been scared by the creatures on the island, but also fascinated to see them for herself. Before Benny came, she was the only person who enjoyed talking about the types of dinosaurs with Alex.

"Sue? Oh no, not Sue," said Alex as he caught his breath and tried to stay calm.

Hearing her name, Sue shivered violently and tried to roll over, whining as she did so. Her sweet, intelligent face was grotesquely swollen and was set into a mask of pain and fear. Her eyes leaked watery blood, and her swollen lips struggled to form words. She was barely recognizable.

Helen wanted to comfort her, but Sue's skin was blistered and leaking blood, so touching her might have hurt her. All around Sue's head was blood-soaked vomit.

As Helen looked around, she decided that whatever killed Durango had caused Sue's condition, as well. "Sue? Can you hear me?"

"Helen?" asked Sue, whose usually soft eyes were shiny and roved madly as she tried to focus, blinking away bloody tears.

"I'm here. It's Helen. You're with friends now."

"Alex? What's wrong with her? The compys aren't bothering her or Durango's body. That's strange." Scott heard the compsognathus chittering as they danced, almost hidden behind the trees, but they didn't come close. Usually, they were curious scavengers.

Alex watched the little dinosaurs. Being the size of large chickens or turkeys, they were always the first to find a free meal and didn't care if the prey were dead or dying. Normally in a pack, they wouldn't hesitate to attack Sue and Durango, but now, were nervously avoiding them. Even with other packs hunting nearby, they were likely to sun, grab a few bites, and retreat, but they didn't bother anyone or anything.

Scott looked at Sue carefully and jerked back, his eyes wide. He looked around and stomped his feet. "Hell, no, look at her."

Helen was perplexed and asked, "What?"

"Snakes. Sue, were there snakes?"

She nodded, tears running down her face.

Helen saw the fang marks and understood the blistering. The marks were small and numerous. "Baby snakes? A nest?"

"Vipers, fer-de-lance," said Sue as she gasped. She slurred the words, but they were clear enough to make sense. She was a smart woman and had identified the type of snake that had bitten her.

Alex frowned. He took the information in and tried to process what Sue was telling him. "No shit? Vipers?" Sue's determination to tell them the information, despite blistered lips, was chilling.

Sue opened her hand, and there in her fist lay a dead baby viper. She had crushed it as it bit her several times on her palm, so swollen that it looked ready to burst. The snake was muddy brown with a pale, creamy yellow belly. It wasn't snake-shaped as people thought of snakes, but had a separate head from its body. It was like a sock that had a ball in the toe with an indentation right before the head began.

The little snake was young, yet its head was broad, and it had a lot of venom. It was likely that Sue and Durango stepped into the midst of a nest of the creatures.

"The fer-de-lance isn't natural to all islands with jungles. I can't say it's a mystery why they are here, yet, it seems strange to find them here, very unique," Alex said.

"Very strange?" Helen asked.

"Not supernatural. Unusual is all."

"No *stranger* than dinosaurs," Scott said. He raised his feet anxiously, watching for the brown snakes to slither from the leaves, but the area was clear as far as he could see. He used a branch to turn the leaves over and look under sticks. "I don't see any."

"They left."

Helen looked into Sue's eyes and asked, "The snakes and the others?"

"Pam. Idiot. She ran to the water for a bath..." Sue struggled to talk, and blood leaked from her mouth. "They got her, I think."

"Dinos?"

"Yeah. Snakes gone?"

"I think so," Helen said. She looked up at the rest, "There's nothing we can do, is there?"

"Paralysis, blisters, and bleeding. People usually don't have these kinds of reaction. I mean, usually when the vipers bite, the symptoms take longer to show, but these things bit them dozens of times, so I think maybe the snakes must have been a little different. Maybe the venom acts faster. Who knows, considering this crazy island?" asked Alex since he wasn't sure. He was smart, he knew a lot of trivia, but he didn't know everything, so he struggled to make sense of the situation. He wished he knew more.

"Can't we..." Bobby shook his head and knelt, taking Sue's hand and speaking softly.

Helen stood with the other four, giving Bobby and Sue privacy.

As she watched the compys running around, she thought about how good the creatures tasted when cooked, kind of like chicken, or frog legs, but she never trusted them. "Why are they avoiding Sue and Durango?"

"Venom. I guess the creatures don't want to eat anything infused with the venom. Sue and Durango may be poisoned now...their skin and other places. I don't know for sure about them. I'm guessing," Alex said. "Where did the snakes go?"

"Deeper into the trees. Under logs. They don't want to be eaten by the compys. They usually avoid humans, so I think Sue and Durango must have stepped right into the nest, and the snakes reacted. Bastards," said Alex as he shivered. "I hope the compys ate them...the snakes...I mean."

In a few minutes, Bobby, his face sad but composed, stood and said, "She's gone. She did say the others ran away from the snakes." Bobby was normally positive, but he looked troubled at losing someone to a new threat. He couldn't keep up with all the dangers on the island. "She was ready to die. She was brave."

"All of them ran deeper into the jungle?" RJ asked.

"Yes, except for Pam. She wasn't here to be bitten. She had run to the spring. I guess the rest ran this way, and two were bitten. I suppose we can follow the trail through the greenery that they left," Scott said. He was undecided and worried.

Tyrese and Davey must have been very afraid for them to leave Durango and Sue. "I think if anyone else had been bitten, they wouldn't have gone far."

Why did Tyrese and Davey run?

"They would be dying or already dead, too. It isn't like Tyrese and Davey to run away, but how could they fight snakes? Right?" Helen asked. She was thinking the same as Scott.

Scott considered the situation and shivered. The others panicked when they walked into the nest of vipers, but Tyrese and Davey were almost fearless. For them to have left Sue, run away from Pam, and not saved her was confusing. He thought he was missing something vital.

"Something feels wrong," RJ said.

"Besides snakes? I hate snakes," Helen said. Scott reached for her hand and tried to give her a reassuring smile, but it became a grimace. "What is it?" she asked since she felt that Scott and Alex were a step ahead in thinking.

Alex tilted his head and narrowed his eyes with admiration, balanced with fear and said, "We're being hunted."

Chapter 4: Extreme Hunting

Helen's face drained of color as she asked, "What do you mean?"

"I mean the compys aren't here because they don't want venomous flesh; they're nervous. See how they keep running back and forth? Those snorts and roars that we heard toward the water sounded like bigger predators, but remember that I said I thought there could be two packs hunting. I still think that."

"Are we being watched, do you think?"

"Maybe. Probably. I have a really bad feeling, and we need to get out of here," Alex said. "They have to be a smaller predator, and remember, we've seen troodons."

"Those are the smart ones. They scare me," Helen said.

"Me, too. They are fast, smart, and sneaky, aren't they? They work in perfect synchronization, something scientists have hypothesized about. They're like the cheetahs of the dino world, I suppose."

"What should we do?"

"I'm not sure. We're moving away from their nest if they are troodons, farther away from camp and water, and farther from the rocks and cave. I don't know where the rest ran, but we don't have a choice since something big is behind us."

"Meaning?"

"I mean that I think the troodons are close and are hunting us, but I think they are as nervous as the compys, because another bigger predator has come into this territory to hunt and has unbalanced everything."

"A lot bigger?"

Alex nodded to Helen and said, "I think it's a lot bigger, but the good news is that it will go back that way to its territory where it belongs."

"What's the bad news?" Bobby asked.

"It's the same way Tyrese and the rest ran, and the way we are heading. The troodons are herding us in that direction."

"Why?"

"Because they want us first. The other territory is like a wall they are backing us into, a dead end. Let's just say that I think they are troodons. They are close, and they want us. Okay?"

"Yeah, thanks, Alex, great news."

Bobby smiled kindly and said, "At least we know. That's something, and we're still alive. We have a chance." He looked to Scott and Alex and said, "And you two can come up with good plans."

"I can come up with a plan, but it might not be very good," Scott said.

Alex took the lead, motioning the rest to follow. He stopped, and they ate from the trees, picking a fruit that Air Marshal Lynn's group had lived on and called *peachy tarts.* As glucose hit her bloodstream from her having eaten some of the fruit, Helen looked a little stronger and seemed to be energized. They gathered the fruit to put in their packs.

"I love these fruit," Alex said.

"One of the only good things we've found," Scott agreed.

"I've packed a lot for us," Helen said.

As they continued on, they noticed the ground was scratched up, looking as if a fight had ensued, and Scott pointed out blood streaks on a few leaves. The biggest carnivores hadn't been there, but either the troodons had a violent fight among themselves, or else, the troodons and humans had a nasty, brutal battle.

"Oh, Alex," said Helen as she waved him over. In a slight depression in the ground lay a dinosaur, four feet long and partly covered with brush where it had fallen. The animal was bluish grey, its skin looked pebbled, and its vestiges of feathers never quite developed, but could have, and might, if evolution occurred.

Covered in tiny feathers, its fuzzy forearms ended with dagger-like claws. The back legs were muscular with its toes tipped with regular claws. In the middle of the foot was a uniquely raised claw, common to most raptors. The head was large, indicating a big brain, and its eyesight was excellent. It wasn't bottom-heavy. In fact, it looked as if it could run and maneuver easily.

"It's a kind of a troodon, I think. Maybe. It's not a velociraptor because it's too big. It's nearly as tall as I am," Alex said. "It may be something totally different, but troodon is as close as I can guess, based on his lizard head, back claws, and tail."

Bloodied, the creature had been stabbed and gouged repeatedly. Again, it was unusual for the compys not to scavenge this fresh meat, but Alex said he thought it was because the pack was still too close. "They'll come for him, his own kind will. We're just in the way right now, and they're watching."

"Keep walking," Scott said, "because I feel them watching. It's creepy as hell."

A large fern with lacey, whitish fronds and pulpy stems exploded, sending bits of greenery into the air. Alex spun with his knife, and Scott jumped forward, but RJ rolled with a blue-grey beast on top of him. The violent thrashing tore the greenery to shreds, and the animal was so fast that no one could find a way to stab it without hurting RJ. The man and beast rolled over rotten logs and against a fallen tree. The dinosaur slashed once, opening RJ's stomach and chest.

Helen screamed with horror as she saw the belly wound. It had happened so fast.

"Run," Scott ordered. Feeling pity and guilt, Scott didn't want to leave RJ, but as he yelled, two other animals burst from the trees where they were hidden, snapping and tearing at RJ and fighting over the kill. Scott wanted to get the rest to safety and then help him, but it didn't happen that way.

One troodon bit into RJ's stomach and yanked his intestines free, pulling a string with him as he retreated. The man screamed and shrieked until the noise became a high-pitched cacophony among the snapping and growls. If Scott went closer, one of the animals would use a back claw to rip him open. Scott wanted to vomit as guilt overwhelmed him.

Scott grabbed Helen before she fell, having just tripped on a vine. Blindly they ran, following a trail that others had taken, but not knowing if it were a trap or a safe zone.

Chapter 5: In the Maw

"Helen, come here, or you're dead. Hurry. "
While Helen ran with the rest to a rocky area, she heard her name and twisted to her left, wondering where the voice came from and whose voice it was.

At the rocky area, grey boulders and stones stood covered with moss and were almost invisible against the ferns and trees, but the smashed plants led that way.

More rocks lined a gully and led off into a cave-like trail where trees and bushes grew, leaning and forming a dark tunnel of over growth.

During storms, the gully always filled with water, and sure enough, thunder and lightning were already rumbling and breaking up the sky.

The sky wasn't yellow tinted yet, as it often became on the island, but the storm was filled with heavy rain clouds, something common for the jungle. A light breeze cooled the air.

Helen didn't have time to look at the gully for very long because a hand reached out from the rocks and yanked her through a slash in the rocks, a crevice that was impossible to discern. She looked up at Tyrese who gripped her arm and pulled her inside the cave and behind him.

She hardly had time to give him a whisper of thanks before she was at the back of the crevice and she had fallen on the damp ground. A soft body broke her fall.

"Ouch, damn," John Littleton complained. John pushed Helen, and Tyrese pushed her back, so she was tossed back and forth.

"Stop it," Helen screamed. Littleton wedged himself into a smaller area and gave her room to squat. She had bumped her head and winced as her scalp began stinging. She felt of her head with gentle fingers and found a small scrape that smarted, but it wasn't serious.

"Don't push me. I cut my head," she snapped at Littleton.

"You startled me."

"Fine, but stop pushing."

Scott slid through the rocks a split second after Alex. It just happened that they were in that order. He turned to help Tyrese pull Bobby into the little cave but realized he was holding a hand and wrist that dripped blood. Scott's yell was full of fury and the agony of frustration and defeat. "Come on. Dive in, Bobby."

"I..." Bobby moaned.

One of the troodons rammed Bobby just as he tried to get inside the crevice and used its knife-like maw to snap his powerful jaws down on the exposed arm. Bobby screamed and spun, unsure where to run. He could have been saved, but a second troodon aggressively raced to the man and bit into his face, tearing away Bobby's eyes and nose. Bobby gurgled a scream.

Bobby took several steps the wrong way and collapsed, screaming in pain. The first troodon chomped down on Bobby's neck, killing him instantly. The animals fought over this kill, ripping away chunks of flesh and tearing off arms and then legs. They snapped at one another as they ate Bobby. They dragged him away, still fighting.

"No...Bobby? We have to do something..."

"He's gone, Scott. You know that. Good Lord, it's as if he gave you the second you needed to be safe. Fine man, wasn't he?" Tyrese watched the rain begin to fall, washing away blood as soon as it welled. "I can't believe we lost him...this close to being safe..."

Scott caught his breath and wiped his face, rubbing away sweat and tears of anger. He wasn't sure that when people were heroic and died, if that action made them better or worse than those who escaped death.

"What the hell? Tyrese, damn, are you okay?" asked Scott, as he ducked away from a spot above him that allowed rainwater to trickle down and fall on his back. "We were worried."

"I think so. Kind of."

"What happened?"

"We screwed up. Everyone was too loud, and Pam ran to the water as if she was on vacation. There was nothing to worry about, but then some big thing got her, we think," Tyrese said.

Benny had a line between his eyes as he concentrated and explained in a calm voice, "The dinosaurs that got Pam…they were ceratosaurus, I believe. They have the horns on their heads and are not carnotaurus because of the size and shape of the upper body. They are smaller than an allosaurus, which is their natural enemy. I don't think this island can support anything much larger than the ceratosaurus."

"Yeah, *Sarah-saurs,* and they are big," Tyrese said, "and I'm so sorry about Bobby. He was a good person."

"Yeah, he was." Despite his horror at losing Bobby, Scott was fascinated to hear about the large dinosaurs. He told Benny about the dinosaur they called Big Brown, a large predator with blue-tipped feathers. They had already killed the female of the species.

Benny nodded and said, "I bet he is one of the last of his kind. A lake or big body of water is probably in that direction. Ceratosaurus like to swim and catch fish. I mean, that's the theory. That is their hunting ground, but pretend the spring and creek are the center. The ceratosaurus came from the other way and hunted in the center of the spring."

"And they got Pam?"

"We heard her scream, and we saw them, so we can assume so," Littleton added. His eyes were enormous. "No one helped her."

"Did you?"

"Well. No."

"We ran this way. We planned to go back down the trail to camp, but the other things were there. Those things," Tyrese said.

"A kind of troodon," Benny supplied the information.

"I knew it," Alex told them, "and they have to be troodons. I am glad you know your stuff."

Benny smiled sadly and said, "Tyrese said the troodons have nests on the other side of the spring. Today, troodons and ceratosaurus decided to hunt in the same area, and unfortunately, we were right in the middle."

"You know a lot about them," Scott said. "In fact, Alex said the same thing."

"I like those creatures, but I don't care for them as much now that they are hunting us. I guess I hate some of them...those that kill people.

I used to read about them, and Dad...Dad was so cool. He took us to all the dinosaur museums and let me take all the junior programs. I loved learning about them and thought about being a paleontologist," said Benny as he sniffed. "I wish Dad could have seen them here."

"You could be the best in the field," Scott said, "and I know you miss your father. I'm sorry, Benny."

"Me, too. I'll be okay. Time heals, right?"

"I hope so," Scott said.

Helen sat in the cramped space and looked at Shonna, who lay on the dirt; she brushed a large yellow-green spider away from Shonna's hair. The bandage on Shonna's arm was thick, having been neatly wrapped with gauze upon gauze, but still the wound leaked blood. "Did you do the medical work, Davey?"

"Yeah, I tried."

"What happened to her? Not the snakes?" Helen was suddenly afraid Davey had removed Shonna's arm because of a snakebite.

"No, the troodons. Her hand is gone, and I can't stop the bleeding. They ripped it off her...horrible. Some of that blood is from a bite on her thigh, likely very deep. The back claw got her. Probably if the wound had been any deeper, she would have died right there. She's in deep shock and hasn't been conscious yet."

"Makes you wish you had your stash of dope?" Helen asked.

"I wish that every day, actually. I need a fattie."

"Drug talk? Really? In front of a kid?"

"It's okay, Uncle John. I guess I've seen and heard worse. Marijuana does have some benefits."

"He's not a kid. He's a teenager and about to mature fast or die out here, so rethink that part," Scott growled.

"Scott..." Helen gulped and took a deep breath.

"Enough," said Littleton as he held his hand up.

"That may be for the best that she hasn't awakened," Helen said. "I know you tried. Except for Kelly, you are the best with first aid, Davey."

"Nah, I'm not half as good as Kelly, and I don't have anything to work with or the room to maneuver." He caught that he had dropped his trademark way of speaking and added, "Dude."

Helen shook her head. She knew Davey wasn't the stoner, the dumb person he pretended to be. He was smart, but he turned to his trademark slang when he grew nervous. She knew that he was frustrated with an inability to make Shonna well and that he feared trying but failing.

Scott explained that they had found Durango and Sue, and had figured out vipers had killed them. Tyrese looked miserable and said he felt like a coward for running and leaving them, but he had wanted to save Benny, who was young. Tyrese's face showed that he didn't like making choices about who lived and who died. "Snakes. Damn things were crawling all over the place."

"Deadly snakes," Alex agreed.

"Bobby was with Sue when she passed. Stu and the rest are going to take the death of Durango hard. I can't believe he's dead. He was always so loud and strong...the central focus...bigger than life," Scott said. "I wanted Durango to lead, and he would have if things hadn't gone the way they did."

"I know. I would have preferred for him to lead as well," Tyrese said.

"You did the best you could. There were snakes..."

"I know. Those baby snakes, God, Scott, you should be glad you didn't see those bastards slithering and crawling all over, and then they just came at us...attacked. I've never seen anything like it...that many together and that many so aggressive," Davey said.

"A nest," Alex said.

"Sons of bitches bit Durango all over his legs, and when he fell, damn, Sue, we just ran. I've never been so scared. There was nothing we could do but run," said Tyrese as he shivered.

"They were gone, but Sue killed one. Fer-de-lance, I think." Alex whispered the name of the snake as if they might hear him.

"Those are native to jungles but not to all of the islands," Benny said. "I think it's rare to see them here, but then, the entire island is weird."

Alex asked the boy what he thought about the venom acting so fast. It was as if the venom were ten times as strong and killed twenty times as fast. Normally, there would be blistering and some hemorrhaging and then necrosis of the bitten area. Some died after being bitten, but other people survived and had to deal with the loss of a limb as it rotted. Alex enumerated his points on his fingers as he talked.

"I have no idea, Alex. Some things here don't fit the science I learned. Things break rules. People die," Benny said as he blinked away tears.

He was intelligent, but he was young, scared, and upset, too. He felt frustrated by the creatures that broke the rules he had learned and that didn't act according to what science taught. It was a betrayal.

Tyrese shoved his long knife out from the rocks where he hid, and a troodon squealed and retreated. Blood covered the blade. "Those things are persistent."

"They hunted us. If Alex hadn't figured it out, we'd all be dead," said Helen, who felt as if spiders were crawling on her, and she batted away a beetle that came too close. She hated the little crevice, but the alternative wasn't pleasant, either. The ground was wet as the water rose to an inch before turning into mud when they stepped in it.

"We can't stay here," John Littleton said. "I didn't believe you...my mistake. When I saw..."

"I know," Helen told him, "and we told you, but until you see *them*, it's hard to believe."

"I didn't know," Littleton said.

Helen asked, "Why did all of you come out here, Ty?"

Tyrese frowned and said, "It was me, Davey, Sue, and Littleton. We wanted him to see a few compys, but everyone else demanded to go with us. I failed as a leader. I told you I couldn't do it, Helen."

"I tagged along. I followed them, and Kelly told me not to," Benny admitted, "but *dinosaurs*. The island is like a dream and a nightmare. Pam said we could explore."

"I know it was bad to see everything this way," Alex said.

"Tyrese saved us, I mean the *us* who are here. He tried hard, but we were pretty scared," Benny said.

He droned on about his theories, lulling them as he spoke. He said he found it strange that there was a large predator population, but a smaller plant eater population. Benny said that the eco-system was wrong, but he didn't know how the island worked. He theorized that meat eaters preyed on one another, but the largest couldn't survive on that and would die out. In time, he said, troodons would be the major predators.

"They're smart, you know. We're smarter, but it's their territory, so we need to think like them, but better."

Alex thought about that. With a stick, he drew in the dirt. "The gully. They'll chase us, but we can fight back. We might make it. Can you see? The water is rushing that way, and I am sure it's filling the gully like a huge water slide."

"Make it where?"

"To the ceratosaurs' territory. If the troodons follow us, they'll be eaten. Maybe they'll be afraid of them anyway. How do you know there is a lake that way, Benny?"

Benny chuckled, "Alex, you're good at this. Do you not know? Jeez. Ceratosaurs are built for swimming with their crocodile bodies and tails. The gully washes right to the lake. They are bigger, but we can stab them just as easy."

"Bigger?" Helen asked.

"We can't leave Shonna," Tyrese said, "because she will be like a dinner bell when they smell blood."

Everyone went quiet, listening to the storm.

"It's okay. She's gone," Davey told them abruptly. "We need to go."

Helen paused a second, looking at Davey carefully and remembered that Shonna had been in terrible condition and would have died, no doubt. However, her heartbeat had been steady before Davey checked her again.He wiped her face while his back was turned so Helen couldn't see Shonna in the dim, watery light.

She wondered if Davey had learned too much from Kelly about making life and death choices. She also wondered about a few others of their group who had been suffering and suddenly died.

It wasn't really as if she knew how she felt about the possibility that Davey helped Shonna along. There was absolutely no hope for the woman, and if she had awakened, the pain and fear alone would have been hellish for her.

Also, waiting for her to die would have kept them in the crevice for a long time, maybe until dark when it would have been too late to escape.

Helen tried to catch Davey's eyes, but he kept his face averted and looked as if losing Shonna hurt him.

A loud burst of thunder shook their little cave. More water ran past the entrance, and they heard it flowing into the gully over the noise of the storm.

"Ahh-eeee," screamed Shonna as she jerked up to a sitting position, scaring Tyrese so badly that he scraped his arm as he jerked.

Helen grabbed Benny's arm and clamped her fingers down tightly, causing him to yelp. Helen's eyes bulged as she hissed, "You said she was dead."

Davey went white, his face doughy in the little bit of light they had, and he shook his head furiously as he moaned, "She was. She was dead and gone, *Dude*. Oh shit, she *isn't* dead."

Chapter 6: Life and Death

"That's what you get for all the damned dope you've smoked, idiot," Tyrese snapped. He rarely was so rude to the survivors, but his heart was hammering. "What the hell just happened?"

Helen pushed her way to Shonna and raised a hand to cover Shonna's mouth, but stopped. *Was she going to cover the horrible squealing noise coming out Shonna's mouth or do something worse?*Helen's hand hovered.

Davey leaned into Shonna's face, "Shut up, or they'll come after us. They can hear noises like…yanno…"

"Pain. They'll come for the blood and because she sounds wounded," Alex said.

"She *is* wounded."

"I know that," Alex told Scott, "and I was explaining." He looked faintly hurt.

"I know. I'm sorry. Damn. Helen, what can we do?"

Davey was already speaking softly and trying to soothe Shonna who lay back, shaking badly and contorting with her pain. She started to scream as she saw the bright red wrappings that ended at her wrist, but Davey slapped a hand over her mouth, glancing at Helen as he did.

"You lost the hand. Be still so you don't bleed anymore," Davey told Shonna.

Helen only nodded as she said, "Shonna, listen to Davey. You have to be quiet or…" She didn't know how to finish her warning and swallowed hard. Whether she was right or wrong about what she thought Davey had done before, she wished Shonna never had awakened in agony, never screamed, and never caused the conundrum they had. She laid a hand on Davey's shoulder and hoped that either way, he understood she felt bad.

"What are we going to do?" Littleton asked.

"*We?*" asked Tyrese as he spun around. "I have yet to see you swing a knife or stab anything. The last thing we need is for someone to ask what we need to do. Shut up, or give me a solution."

"Ty, calm down. You know that I led people out here to find you guys because I was afraid some from the group came along with you who weren't very tough. I lost RJ and Bobby, and I feel that's on me. You can't give up and let the anger take you. You aren't responsible for each person," Scott said.

Tyrese rubbed his eyes. He had the saddest expression that Scott had ever seen.

"I shouldn't have let them tag along. I should have made them act right on the trail. I should have stopped Pam. I should have never let everyone run into the jungle...right into the damned snakes. The rest...I tried hard," said Tyrese.

"I know you did. This is a bad spot, but we can do as Alex and Benny said. We have to outsmart the monsters and get back to the beach," Scott spoke, but tried to imagine how they would have to get fresh water day after day and face the same situations. This was about far more than getting back to the beach, but for now, it was all he could think of. The idea of a twelve-year-old like Benny being eaten alive was impossible to consider.

"Shonna, can you walk? Can you run? Because we have to run," Davey said.

Shonna lay back, shivering and said, "I can't stand the pain."

"She can't run. With that gash, she can't walk," Helen said.

Davey sat back and said, "Her wrist is bleeding badly, and the gash in her leg is bleeding almost as much. I can't fix her, there's nothing for pain, and she's going to draw the dinos. Someone, tell me what to do. *Anyone*. I can't do this alone."

Shonna squealed again. Her eyes rolled madly, and she thrashed in the tight space. No one answered Davey.

"We have to think of something," Littleton said, risking Tyrese's anger.

"I'm trying," Davey replied, "so all of you go, and I'll stay with her. Maybe we'll be okay, and then tomorrow, you can come back and get us." Davey shrugged and then said, "We can survive. Probably."

"That's workable," John Littleton agreed.

Scott raised a hand before Tyrese could move. "We didn't ask you. There's no way Davey could defend himself and Shonna if even a few small troodons got in here." Scott stabbed a large beast in the nose as it peeked inside the crevice, and enjoyed the squeal it emitted as it ran away.

Outside the crevice, the troodons ran back and forth, growling and trying to find a way to get at their prey, but also aware that the humans could harm them. So far, the troodons had used a hunting method of knocking their prey down and biting, which worked for human-sized prey and worked well all that day.

The troodons' *food* was hidden in a rock crevice, which frustrated them. They knew their hunting time might be limited because of the other, larger beasts hunting in the area.

Each troodon had a sickle-shaped claw on each of his feet, a blade that was six inches long and lethal. The creatures were capable of raising their feet and clawing open flesh easily. When they attacked a larger animal, they leaped and slashed.

Intelligent and clever as well, several of the larger troodon, the alphas or leaders, began to use a few rocks that lay almost buried in the ground, covered by rotting vegetation and moss to frighten their prey.

Click-click-click.

Trying to intimidate or scare the prey from the rocks, they tapped and hissed. The resulting noise was terrifying.

Birds and lizards ran away, the compys retreated, and the humans trembled.

No one had to ask Benny or Alex what was happening. The constant clicking grew unnerving.

Scott outlined a plan asking Alex what he thought. It wasn't a perfect plan, and it wasn't to everyone's liking, but they had to do something. If they didn't return to camp, more of their group might come looking for them and walk into the trap the troodons had set.

"We're just leaving her? You said some of those could sneak in here. Will she be okay? We'll come back for Shonna?" Benny asked.

"Sure, soon as we can," Scott lied.

"We won't, but I understand. It's all about who it is, right? Because if it were Helen," Littleton said.

"Stop," Scott said. He felt his face go red, and he turned away from the rest. "At some point, we have to stop people from dying."

"The one as opposed to the many?" Benny asked. His voice was innocent. There was no malice, but his words cut as deeply as a troodon's claw.

"Davey, are you checking on Shonna? Keeping her quiet?" Scott wanted to scream with frustration. He had no ideas and was terrified that Helen might die in the little cave as well.

"Give me a minute. Damn. Shit. Scott, I can't..." Davey said.

"Do you want me to do it?" Scott asked.

"Do what?" Littleton asked.

"Nothing," Davey mumbled.

"She can't run or walk. We can't possibly carry her, can we?" Helen asked. She knew what Scott meant. She had thought the same thing as Scott had.

"*We* can't. *I* can. I'll carry her," Tyrese said. "If we can get out of here without being attacked and you can raise her and position her without her bleeding out, I can carry her. Help me get her up, Davey, and I can do it. You better not move too slow, or we'll all die."

"Can you swim, Benny?" Helen asked.

"Yes, ma'am, I'm a good swimmer."

"You'll need to be. Keep your arms up to protect your head and keep your legs bent and kick off the rocks, understand?"

"So it isn't about swimming as much as it is about dodging rocks? Got it," said Benny as he nodded.

Designated as point guards and ready with knives, Alex and Helen ran out from the rocks first.

Nothing chased them because both were fast, dodging into the brush quickly, and then the gully, using the rain as a shield. They jumped into the water and were carried along quickly, as the current of the water was strong. Benny and John Littleton followed, trying to keep up. Both splashed into the gully and were swept down stream.

Davey and Scott yanked Shonna out of the safe area and up, and then they threw her over Tyrese's shoulder so he could carry her in a fireman-carry. She cried as her thigh hit his chest, and the pain flared. Tyrese ran, following the rest.

Davey and Scott guarded the back of the group in the direction they feared an attack would come.

Tyrese strained as he eased himself into the water, but the bank rumbled, and he and Shonna fell. He held her tightly.

Scott panicked as the clicking of the sickle-claws stopped and the bushes began to flutter with dashing troodons.

A medium-sized creature jumped at the gully, trying to knock Scott down and rip him open with its claws.Scott stayed under the branches, ducked, and stabbed at the animal as it missed him. Scott only wounded the dinosaur, blood staining some of the muddy froth.

The pack, snapping and clawing, smelled blood from the injured beast as well as from Shonna and went into a frenzy. Because of the fast moving current, Scott was swept safely past the creature.

The confusion gave the humans a few seconds of advantage. Everyone dodged rocks, kicking off when necessary, but Tyrese struggled with Shonna.

In another lifetime, in a place where dinosaurs didn't roam, Shonna was a man who felt he should have been born a woman. The surgeries were done well, and only one man knew the facts and had shared, but that situation made no difference to anyone, except for now.

Male or female, Shonna was tall and had solid muscles, making her an attractive woman, but also showing she was heavy. Tyrese was a large man, strong and muscular, but he struggled with Shonna's weight.

He fought to protect Shonna's head as he held her above water. She hit a crop of rocks and screamed as they bruised and cut her stomach. Her stump bled freely in the water and throbbed because of her position. She cried.

Scott caught his breath as he grasped a branch next to Tyrese and asked, "You want me to hold her?"

"You aren't that big," said Tyrese as he grinned. He whirled as a troodon jumped down through the brush and caught his arm, cutting it deeply with its claw. The splash covered the human's heads for a second, but the troodon fought to get to its prey.

Scott stabbed, but in seconds, smaller beasts jumped down, and using their smaller, but dexterous forelegs, they snapped at Tyrese.As he spun, Shonna's body took the damage, something Tyrese didn't intend, but again happened because of her position.

She went under and came up spitting and sputtering but wasn't able to do more than wave her arms weakly. Tyrese covered his face and neck as the animals swam to him, and he tried to use the fast current to get away.

Davey skewered one with his pike, but couldn't pull the weapon back out to use again; it was stuck fast. The water gave him no traction. He then pulled his knife from his belt.

Benny yelled with fear as an animal leaned down from the bank of the gully and snapped at him. Helen and Alex stabbed and stabbed, finally wearing themselves out. Stabbing hard flesh was tiring, and in the hot jungle where they poured sweat as they fought, they dehydrated.

Scott knocked the second of the animals off Tyrese, but it still wanted to kill and eat Tyrese and Shonna. Tyrese yelled and clutched his stomach. Benny waved his arms to distract the beast, and Alex and Scott slashed. The dinosaur swam to the edge of the gully and scuttled up, wounded.

Davey leaned over, looked at Shonna, and said to no one in particular, "She's *really* dead. I think she bled out or hit her head on one of those rocks."

Helen robotically felt for a pulse. "We need to keep swimming and follow this thing to the lake. Ty, Hon, you have to let her go."

"I...let her go?"

"Yeah, let her go. She's gone for real this time."

Tyrese moaned and let Shonna go, watching her body spin, bounce, and go under a few times as she floated away. For some reason he said, "I'm sorry, Benny."

"Me, too," Benny said as he gasped for breath.

"You're doing great, Dude. Stay sharp," Davey said.

"Stay under the branches," Scott ordered. "I think we're close to something." The scent of the jungle was different even in the gully. They could smell dead fish and algae. He hoped they could skirt the lake and wind back to the beach and then to camp.

"Holy shit."

No one corrected Benny's language because all of them felt the same, as they came out next to a somewhat mushy, muddy beach. The well- trampled beach was littered with pebbles and covered by the same kind of rocks that made the cave the humans had hidden in. Heavy footprints marked the muck that smelled of rotting fish and reptilian feces. A sharp, bitter reek was evident as the mud soured.

Helen twisted her hair, trying to get the dirty water out so it would stop dribbling down her back.

In the murky water of the lake, a ceratosaur swam, using its stout tail to propel itself across the surface while its head was half submerged as it searched for fish. In the creature's wake, swam several smaller dinosaurs, mimicking the swimming motions and learning the fishing technique. Seeing them work together was amazing, but surreal, as if watching a movie.

"We can stay in the trees and angle back to the beach. Stay together," Scott warned. "Benny and Alex were right. The troodons have backed away from us."

"They fear the ceratosaurs," Benny said.

"I do, too," Alex said.

Davey took some gauze from Helen's backpack to wrap Tyrese's wounds. That the gauze had remained dry was shocking, but so far, small plastic bags worked to keep their belongings dry in their backpacks. In time, there would be none of those left.

"Keep Ty, Benny, and Littleton in between us," said Scott.

"I can still kick ass, Scott," Tyrese grumbled. As much as guilt ate at him, he was still brave and determined; something the rest admired. He held out his knife and looked around. "I feel bad for Shonna."

"You tried, Ty. I was impressed," Benny said. He admired Tyrese's dedication and bravery.

Scott almost grinned as he watched his friend. He was stopped from his mirth as John Littleton stumbled and moaned when his ankle turned. "Don't tell me about a sprained ankle. We don't have time for that," said Scott.

"I wouldn't dream of telling you," Littleton scowled. He felt outside the group but noticed that Benny fit in perfectly.

A roar echoed, and then there was a discordance of bellowing, squealing, thrashing, and cracking. The troodons ventured too close to the ceratosaurs' territory, and the two packs fought over the food and the land.

Several of the troodons, working together as a team and using their sickle-shaped back claws, could sometimes bring down a ceratosaur, but because that was so deadly to try, it wasn't a common fight. They preferred to use their abilities to attack a plant-eater who couldn't fight back as well.

The ceratosaurus had the huge, sharp teeth that herbivores didn't have, and they snapped bones and tore flesh, splashing the plants and trees with gore.

The fight between the two packs broke out near the water, coloring the greyish water deep red and the mud maroon. The clashing of so many teeth and bones sent birds and small animals running, while trees were hit so hard that they fell to the waterline.

"It sounds like a war," Littleton said.

"It is," said Alex as he sucked in hot, humid air, trying to make the stitch in his side ease. The air was better than it had been at the small lake but was still sticky and thick.

"I knew our plan would work," Benny told them, "but I wish I could have seen the fight."

"No, you don't because you'd wind up as part of the menu," Helen told him, "and you can't sneak back, so don't even try. You need to learn to fight them if they attack before you run into the jungle. It's fight or die around here."

"I'll learn. How did you get over being amazed, Alex?" asked Benny.

Alex looked startled but replied, "I'm still amazed when I see them. I never dreamed...well, no, that isn't true, because we all dream things like this when we are young, but..."

"We stopped seeing them as interesting and more like enemies. They're nothing more than big snakes to me," Tyrese said. "It's getting late. Do we try to make a camp or push to get home?"

"Are there dinos on the beach?" Littleton asked.

Alex stopped and looked puzzled. "Many of them like the water, and we've been attacked on the beach. Do you just now understand all this?"

"Actually, I don't understand *any* of this. You've had a little longer to accept everything, but it's new to me," Littleton said as he glared at Alex. "Look, I'm trying to get everything in my head, but so far, you've told me, or I have seen that I am five years in the past, so I exist in two places. You have told me about steroid-enriched water that made kids feral, extra venomous snakes and...*shock*... dinosaurs."

"Sorry, dude, but we told you the facts," Davey said.

"We had to find it out for ourselves, so I guess we have sort of a bitterness," Helen explained. "And, yes, there can be dinosaurs anywhere. We don't want to be caught in the dark, though."

They were far to the opposite side of where they had explored before, and camp lay in between. Littleton traced the tree line down the sandy, white beach to the clear water of the ocean. If they were attacked from either direction, they knew that the other way was too far to run and of little value.

"Will those at camp worry if we are out all night?" asked Benny.

"Yeah, I imagine they are already worried, but they'll wait until morning before starting a search party, I hope," Scott said.

"Do you think the rain is finished?" asked Helen.

"If anything, it should be a clear night. No rainstorms," answered Scott.

"Good. I'd hate to reappear again, having already crashed on the beach twice," said Littleton as he grimaced.

Chapter 7: Sand and Bones

Benny's face lit up as he pointed to the line of trees that grew just at the edge of the sand, their roots struggling to find nutrients in the thin, dry soil. Vines reaching around with fingers of green snaked through the trees, trying to find the light. It was as if someone had drawn an imaginary line and the trees had to remain behind it.

Entangled in the vines, but laying on the beach, was a pile of large old bones, twisted and scattered for over twenty yards in each direction and rising several dozen feet high in the middle.

"Big bones." John Littleton wasn't impressed.

"They're huge bones," Alex said. "We haven't seen anything nearly this size." Benny and he stared at the bones, looking side to side and above. With a common interest that chased away fear, they walked around the heap, touching various smooth yellowed surfaces and poking at specific features on the skulls, feet, and spines.

Benny scampered under bones and posed to show his size as if he were being photographed. Alex nodded as he made mental notes of the sizes of the bones.

"What do you think of this one, Benny? What do we have here? Can you tell?"

Benny took the questions to be a test, but was unconcerned about passing because he knew the answers. He referred to the feet of the beast, showing everyone how the long forelegs ended in small hoof-like phalanges. While the huge creature walked mostly on his back legs, he also used his forelegs to walk as well as to feed on both low vegetation and the fruit from taller bushes and trees.

The second point of interest to Benny was the skull of this animal: it was enormous, was shaped like a duck's head, and had large, square teeth. Benny could have slept inside of it, and in fact, he figured he would since they had made camp there.

He pointed to the teeth and said, "See how old they look? They're so worn down and used up…had to be a very old creature.

It was an herbivore and chewed his food, explaining the extreme wear over time."

"Plants wear out teeth?" asked Littleton.

"Sure. It takes a lot of chewing to break down vines and branches and to chew fibrous leaves," replied Benny.

"I agree," Alex said, and Benny nodded, "and the creature must have been about forty feet long and weighed four tons. Do you think it might have been an Edmontosaur?" Alex asked, but was almost afraid Benny would show him up on dinosaur knowledge.

"I think so. If not, it is just like one, or one of the relatives. I still think huge animals can't be living here, for the most part, I mean. He may have been one of the last unless you've seen more?"

"Nothing this size that looks like a duck," Davey said, "but they ate plants, though. That's good."

Benny shook his head and said, "It would be good, but look at this dinosaur that is wrapped up over him. He's just as large, which makes no sense. I think both species died out together since ecosystems need both to balance."

Alex gestured to one of the neural spines on the vertebrae. The boney spine wasn't long enough to suggest a spinosaurus, a very different kind of beast related to the allosaurus, only larger. The spine would have been impressive but not sail-like. "Those spines supported heavy muscles. This guy wasn't just long, forty-five feet or so, he was heavy and powerful. In combat, he could best any of the rest we have seen."

"He was bigger than the Sarah-things?" Littleton asked.

"Ceratosaurus. Yes. Bigger. And meaner," Alex explained. As he spoke, he helped make camp along with the rest. Because they couldn't get back to the main camp before dark, this was the safest place to camp: right inside the tangle of bones, safe within the maze of interlocking, heavy bones of the animals. "We say *mean*, but in reality, it's only the survival of the fittest."

"That could be for humans, too. I'm not sure any humans can hope to survive alongside of dinosaurs. It isn't natural," Benny said.

"I bet you were the smartest kid in your class, huh? You're a sharp guy, Benny," Helen said.

Benny blushed, answering, "I don't know. Maybe. I wasn't very well liked. Kids never like the smart kids."

"I do," Helen told him, "and is your sister smart like you are?"

"Amy? Ha. She is average at best, but she's pretty, so all the kids liked her. Go figure."

"She is pretty, but she'll have to be smart and strong here. You have the advantage. Maybe you can show her."

"I'll try, but, Helen, she's dense at times."

Helen smirked and enjoyed the moment. Scott caught her eyes and smiled back; he liked seeing the rapport she had with Benny. Helen seemed to get along with almost everyone.

Tyrese and Scott dug into the sand to make a place that was lower and one they could defend if necessary, and then they started a fire. While there wouldn't be much water or more than a few scraps of food for the night, at least they would be safe. They hoped. Tyrese stopped his work for a second and asked, "How do you know these things?"

Tyrese had never been one for books and had struggled in college; he admired those who knew things like Benny and Alex did.

"The size is easy," Benny said. "See those teeth? Huge and serrated. There isn't a ridge in front of the eyes like an allosaur, and it has the big eye sockets, see? Allosaurus also have serrated teeth, but they looked very different."

"You went around comparing dinosaur teeth?" Davey asked. "That's cool."

"You didn't?" Benny grinned. "I'm serious, but the spines really give it away. Those and the back legs. Look at those bones."

"Big?" Helen asked.

"Sure, but if we compared them, let's just say that these would be much larger than most meat eaters," said Benny.

"Bigger than a T-Rex?" Tyrese asked. It was his favorite from the movies.

Benny laughed. "Everyone always wants to compare everything to those. In size, allosaurus were similar, I guess. The T-Rex had seven or eight times the bite force of this guy."

Davey said that sounded less terrible to him, but Benny explained that the troodons and ceratosaurus also had a weaker bite force and killed in vicious ways. He didn't know how to explain, so he said it was like deciding whether to be put in a cage with a starving lion, a starving leopard, or a starving catamount. "Each of those would tear you to shreds and eat you. Bite force isn't as important if you're being chewed on by a troodon, and they have better pack-hunting skills. It evens out."

"What do you think it was?" Alex asked. "The meat eater, I mean."

"Acrocanthosaurus, I'm guessing from the features, but Alex, that doesn't fit, does it? All of these dinosaurs? They don't *fit*," Benny said, looking uncharacteristically troubled.

"What does that mean?" Helen asked as they sat around the fire. She wished she had fish to eat, but was scared of their trying to go out into the water after having been so close to death earlier, and afraid the scent would draw predators. Instead, she ate the few fruits they had gathered.

"Dinosaurs appeared millions of years apart. You've heard of Cretaceous and Jurassic? Triassic? Each of those times wasn't just a few thousand years, but was made up of millions of years and subdivided. The dinosaurs we have found are scattered throughout the last millions and millions of years, and in the real world, whatever you call it, they would not have been around each other," Alex said. "Is that what you mean, Benny?"

"Yep. That and the ecosystem, as I said, but also, I'm guessing, like you are, at a few of the types, but we're close on most, I think. Some of these may have been in Canada or some in Texas, and some may be European. The snakes are not usual, either. I'm saying that as far as location, it's as if these things came from all over. There's no general location for all of these things," said Benny.

"Huh?" asked Tyrese.

Helen waved at Tyrese because she understood and needed a second to think. "They don't all belong in any one time or place."

Alex nodded and said, "Exactly."

"The same as we don't belong in *your* time," Benny said. "We belong five years ago.

These belong to a variation of millions of years ago." He frowned as he tried to find the words he needed. He understood his feelings, but an explanation was far more difficult for him. "The time here is watery. Thin," said Alex.

"What does that mean?" Tyrese asked.

Benny shrugged. "I don't know, but maybe out there," he said as he waved in the general direction of the ocean, "it could be a million years ago, or today, or a million years from now. All of us could be here, or all of us may be extinct."

Chapter 8: In the Daylight

In the morning light, Alex and Benny studied the bones more carefully. Benny dug sand away in a specific area, scooping and kicking like a dog, as Alex prodded and poked at the sand, pulling loose shells, stones, and a few grey, arrowhead-shaped rocks that he set to the side. Pieces of rotten wood were added to a pile of material they collected.

"Why are you doing that?" Littleton asked again. He thought that *before when he asked, they said they wondered how the carnivore died, but he didn't understand why it mattered.* He picked up a rock that Alex threw into the pile Benny and Alex were making.

Larger than Littleton's hand, the stone looked flecked and was smooth where bits had been broken away. The end was pointed sharply enough that he pricked his finger as he pressed it. The sides weren't sharp enough to give him a clean shave, but they were lethal enough to cut someone's skin. He saw the rotten wood, and then he picked up long laces that were dried into strands.

"At some point, the laces were maybe hide used to hold a spear tip onto the end of a spear. Wood. Spears. The leather broke free and became sun-bleached, ruined by the water and the years, and telling a story of how this big fellow died," explained Benny.

"It does?" Littleton asked.

"Sure," Benny said, "and the Edmontosaur was grazing here, and the Acrocanthosaur attacked him, but right before that or right at the same time, he was attacked by a different predator. Humans. You can see the nicks on the ribs. I guess he might have been wounded a while before coming here but not too long before. Maybe he was dying and the humans stabbed him here... can't tell the time line."

"Before you ask, I know this answer," Scott said. "It wasn't us. The people from the plane, Air Marshal Lynn's group, didn't hunt here. It's possible the feral kids did this, but..."

"But these bones have been here longer than that. I'd guess close to eight or ten years. That means there have been more people on the island, something we have suspected," Alex said.

"Seems with the wrecks, it should be populated by people running all over the place…like a Mexican resort."

Scott shook his head when Littleton said that. He took Helen's hand as they walked, worried as always that there would come a time when he would not be standing in front of Helen during a dinosaur attack, or that he wouldn't see a nest of snakes, or that something else would kill her. He didn't know how to predict or prevent trouble.

All through the night he sat, watching for shadows and listening for dinosaurs, terrified that all kinds would converge on the beach, hunting them. Scott feared seeing his friends dying and his being left alone more than he feared being devoured.

"We're an endangered species, Littleton," Scott said. "There…look…home."

They hurried down the beach to meet the larger group at the shipwreck.

"What happened? We've been worried about all of you," said Kelly, as she and Stu met the group coming into camp. All of the rest stood close so they could find out where the group had been.

"Where's Dad?" Stu demanded.

"More like where is everyone else? Are they coming separately? Why did you come from that side of the beach? Let me see those cuts," Kelly took Tyrese by the arm and led him to the fire where she could check him over and clean his wounds. "Where is Sue and…"

She stopped asking questions as she saw Tyrese wince, not from the pain of his cuts, but from her questions.

"I asked where my father was," Stu said.

"I heard you. Give us a second. Let us get some water first and food; we're hungry," Scott responded.

"He didn't make it, Stu," Tom said, understandingly.

Joy moved closer beside Tom, still holding his hand. She traded glances with Kelly. For once, Joy and Kelly had similar concerns as they watched Tom's brother, Stu.

"Two packs were hunting close to the creek, and Pam ran right into one of them. The rest had to dodge the larger pack as well as the snakes," said Scott.

Scott glossed over details and made it sound as if Durango and Sue had encountered snakes and died quickly and easily.

Stu didn't react as expected, but the darkness in his eyes eased back, and he nodded as he took a deep breath and said, "He hasn't been well since the wreck. The dad I knew would never have blundered into a nest of damned snakes."

"I doubt he or anyone else would have known there were snakes. Tyrese didn't expect them," Scott said.

Stu turned halfway around as his mother let loose with loud braying sobs, maybe the first real non-dramatic tears of her life. It had taken her a few seconds to face the reality of losing Durango, even if he hadn't been the same since the shipwreck.

For days after the shipwreck, Durango had stared into open space, and then he had started walking again and talking with a heavy slur. Connie had thought he would recover, despite Kelly's saying he had a serious brain injury.

Standing beside Connie, Stu's sister, Vera, listened and picked up a small, feathered dinosaur that she was teaching to eat bits of food like a pet bird, and she walked to the other side of the camp, leaving her mother alone.

Vera was trying to learn to use a bow and arrow, but lost interest within a few days. With the loss of her father, she felt farther away from her accustomed social status. Her eyes were shiny with anger and irritation, as she realized she was becoming more powerless.

She knew dinosaurs cared nothing for her temper tantrums and begging. Her brothers cared far less. So her only interest was in the small dinosaur she thought of as a pet bird. Angus was his name.

"I'm awful sorry, Connie. Vera. Tom. Stu. Vaughn. There was nothing we could do," Tyrese said, "and you know how we loved Durango."

"Thanks, T, I know," Tom said, "but I can't believe there were snakes, too."

"I think they aren't common here or at least not like anacondas and pythons, which we have seen before, but something we still have to be aware of. If vipers can be that venomous, then it's possible...no probable...that there are other snakes here that could be larger and more deadly," Alex said. "For that matter, even bugs could be dangerous."

"Thanks for the nightmares, Alex," said Joy.

"No, don't be that way, Joy. It's better we know this. Maybe there was a reason for Dad's dying. We *know* now," said Stu.

Joy and Tom looked at Stu with shock, yet almost since day one, his moods had bounced around. At times, he had been patronizing and at other times, cruel, sneaky, shockingly angry, and even dangerous.

Tom treaded carefully as he said, "Okay, that's something to consider. Dad would be glad of anything that would help the rest of us."

"That's what I meant," Stu said.

Scott told them the other parts, never focusing on a particular detail. Air Marshal Lynn sat with the rest of his group and hugged Mattie as they learned how RJ and Bobby were killed. "Marshal, they both were heroic, but just didn't make it."

"Both?" Lynn asked.

"Yes, I'm sorry," said Scott.

Mattie spoke up, "All of us survived just fine until we joined your group." Then, Mattie began to cry.

"I know, and I'm sorry for that," Scott said. It was true.

Kelly narrowed her eyes and said, "You survived, but medically, all of you were not healthy. You were pale from lack of sunlight and weak and sickly, along with having rashes. You didn't have any protein." She didn't bother listing their oral blisters, often-bruised skin, stomach problems, and headaches. With a pure fruit diet, they had suffered, but seemed to have forgotten that part. "You weren't doing very well back then."

"It's okay, Kelly," said Scott, knowing she was defending him partly because of the argument between them the morning before. "I'm sorry."

The air marshal rubbed his face and said, "I'm sorry we snapped at you. Mattie is upset. We all are. We cared deeply about RJ and Bobby, and Shonna..."

Mattie looked up. Shonna had been the woman, no the man; no, she was the transgendered person whom her husband had tossed her away for. Mattie and her husband planned to be divorced when they returned from their trip, but their plane crashed. Both Shonna and Mattie broke up with Mattie's husband when he left the plane to go live in the caves. Later, the survivors believed the Utahraptors killed Mattie's husband.

Mattie asked, "Did Shonna die painfully?"

"She was wounded. She lost her hand and was cut on the leg, and I tried to save her, but there wasn't much I could do," Davey said.

Mattie nodded. She didn't wish Shonna pain once she had gotten to know her and found that they were on the same side. They weren't best friends, but Mattie had liked Shonna.

"She was dead and then alive again," Benny reminded them.

Helen interrupted, "We thought she was dead because she was shallow breathing and the little cave was so dark.She moaned, and we knew she was alive, barely. Tyrese carried her out of the cave. We were attacked again, and we lost her in the gully when it filled up with water." Davey gave Helen a thankful look.

Connie walked away to the wreckage of their yacht, *Connie Louise,* and Tom cried for his father a while. After all of them were calm and Scott's group had eaten and hydrated themselves, the group let Benny explain about all the bones they found and the theories he had.

Stu asked several questions, but agreed it was all as insane as he had figured. Benny only confirmed the insanity.

"What about water? We still need..."

Stu interrupted Scott to say, "Harold, the marshal and I went and got it. We knew something bad had happened at the creek because of the way it looked."

The water was cloudy in places because of the fighting in the shallows. In spots, feces, along with rotting pieces of flesh and bones not picked clean, were everywhere, making the water unfit to drink. Deep animal tracks were pressed into the muddy banks, and two ripped up troodon bodies lay at the edge of the water.

"We had to decide if we should go deeper into the jungle or try something else. We followed part of the creek and get *this*, it wound around and around over rocks and seemed to vanish, but then, as we followed the damp ground, we found a new spring," Stu explained by drawing in the sand with a stick.

From the rocks, a spring bubbled, ran down a few feet off rocky ledges, and ended as a heavy drop into a pool. The icy cold water was clear and tasted of minerals.

"The spring also twisted back around the pool, and I have a feeling that is what feeds the nasty swamp, which the troodons and Utahraptors like nesting close to. The main pool is nowhere near, though. It's closer to us than other springs we've found."

Just a little distance down the beach was a slight break in the trees, and not far into the trees was where Stu's trio ended up, surprised that they could almost see the beach from where they were.

"In two trips, we brought back a lot of water, and the spring was far safer than the other place," said Stu as he grinned. "We were able to get everyone there to wash off. The ocean water never felt that clean."

Scott smiled and said, "Smart. It's lucky to have that spring so close. Yeah. I know. Salt water."

"You did a good job, Stu," Scott told him. It was hard to admit, but he needed the group to feel peaceful again. Stu had done a good job in finding water that was closer.

"I always said I could lead if people backed off and let me," Stu said.

"Tyrese leads us," Davey argued, feeling nervous about the direction the conversation was taking.

"Not too well, since my father was killed. How many died with Tyrese leading and you leading, Scott? Too many. I'm not *blaming* you," said Stu.

"Really? It sure sounds like you just did," Scott said. At every turn, Stu wanted to argue with him. He meant his compliment of Stu's discovery of the better spring, and he wanted to work as a team, but the argument was beginning anew.

"I'm saying that too many died. You didn't do smart things. It sounds like Benny has more sense than anyone does. What's your opinion, Mr. Littleton?" asked Stu.

"Ummm, I don't know how things work here. I'm still...well...people were ripped up...like meat...they died," said Mr. Littleton.

"Exactly, and we don't want that. Did anyone ask for your input?" asked Scott.

"Tyrese told me to be quiet, actually," said Littleton.

Stu smiled smugly.

"That's not fair. We were in a bad spot, and someone had to make tough choices," Helen said. "Stu, as we recall, Lori died when you were with her. You aren't perfect."

"That's low. You know damn well what happened."

"Yeah, I know you were attacked and couldn't fight back. I know someone died. Same thing. The thing is shit happens, no matter what." Helen turned to Kelly and asked, "How is Tyrese?"

"He's *lucky*. Davey cleaned his cuts well, and there's no sign of infection. *Lucky,* Mr. Littleton's ankle isn't sprained. It's sore, but there's no real swelling. You were all *lucky*."

Stu, bored with the talking, took his brother Vaughn with him to fish. Harold and Benny's sixteen-year-old sister, Amy, went with Stu. Despite being bruised and having lost her father in the shipwreck, Amy had a positive attitude and was eager to get into the water and learn how to fish.

The cook was excited about his crab traps and promised a big crab dinner, supplemented with scavenged food. He enjoyed providing the best meals he could under the circumstances and was glad the ocean provided for them. A few squid, some fish, and some shellfish would be just what he needed for a stew, slow cooked for breakfast.

The rest worked to secure the wreckage they called home and check the perimeter. The soil showed signs that the feral children had been there spying on the group and that the compsognathus were there also, watching for spoils.

Benny had a novel idea to set up spears or at least sharp sticks in the sand to discourage blitz attacks. He told the rest that although collecting the spore of big meat eaters was disgusting, it would probably also repel smaller carnivores.

"Nasty. We're collecting dino poop," said Tyrese, laughing.

The sky went yellow as the sun set and black-bellied clouds rolled in thickly. Streaks of rain showed on the horizon, and lightning flashed, lighting up the sky over the ocean long before the storm arrived.

Each person in the group stopped at some time and watched the sky with dread and fear. Storms always brought death and more mysteries.

It was a loud, violent storm, and the wind tore at the carefully crafted, woven palm fronds that kept the rain out. The structure shivered and shook in the wind despite its size and weight.

Collected rainwater was always a bonus, but the rain forced everyone to stay inside the wreckage and eat smoked meat and whatever else had already been cooked. In this storm, the rain fell in sheets, making everyone feel damp and miserable.

Stu reminded the group that during storms such as this, shipwrecks appeared on the beach, and pointed out that Littleton and his group was as an example.

"What if I show up a third time?" asked Littleton.

Stu almost laughed but caught himself and frowned, instead. He didn't know what to think after everything he had witnessed. "Let's hope not."

"If I do, I'm going to tell myself to stay out of the damned jungle and watch for snakes."

They heard a strange, high-pitched whistle over the thunder and wind. It grew into a roar that made several of the survivors dare the rain and winds to move so they could see.

In one of the lightning-lit clouds, a dark shadow raced across the sky, familiar and unfamiliar at the same time. The jungle suddenly exploded with light, and the noise became enormous, as if a bomb had gone off somewhere past the spring where they had gotten water before. It was very far away but still bright as it burned.

Helen grabbed Scott and held him as the ground lightly shivered with shock waves. Above the tops of the trees, they could see that a small mushroom cloud rose hundreds of feet in the air. On the wave of air that rushed over the beach was the scent of burning plastic and wood.

"That was an airplane," Stu said, "and that's all the fuel burning up."

"It might have been us," Mattie whispered.

The air marshal frowned and said, "But it wasn't, Mattie. We didn't burn up. It's okay, Hon. We made it."

"I think you're right, Stu. Damn. It must have been a big one. Did you ever know an airliner that big that went missing in The Triangle?" Helen asked.

"No, the marshal and Mattie's flight...that was the biggest I have ever known of that went missing. Do you remember all the media reports? They talked all the time about it on television."

"The media said it was a hijacker or something else, but people couldn't figure out how a jetliner could just vanish like...well, like yours did," Scott said.

"I remember that," Helen told Scott.

"You heard about us? Isn't that weird?" Mattie asked.

"The plane that just crashed has to be bigger than your plane, but how can that be? There is no such thing as *bigger than your plane*?" Stu asked. "This one that just crashed is larger than any we have ever seen in *our* time, yet, we will never know anything about it."

Benny stood with his eyes bright and rain dripping on his face. He was so shocked that he couldn't get his words out and pointed and slapped his leg, trying to explain, "I get it. It hasn't vanished yet, but in my world, neither have you or your yacht. That's a plane that *will* vanish sometime."

Scott and Helen stared at him. Stu tried to talk but sputtered instead.

Alex chewed on a piece of smoked meat and frowned, not happy with the theory; it wasn't complete. A part of the puzzle was missing for him. "Stu, most of the vanishings in the Bermuda Triangle were long ago, right? I mean it did seem that they became fewer as communications improved. The *Violet Marie* was a fluke. The *Connie Louise* is a fluke."

"So?" asked Stu.

"I think when the storms come, they take what they can find at whatever time possible. The storms are hungry," said Alex.

"You've lost it, Alex," said Stu.

Stu watched the flames and was jolted as more violent noises erupted down the beach. This storm was far worse than all before it, and had their yacht been caught in this one, they'd all have died.

"Mark my words, this place is where the storms collect...specimens...victims...things. I don't like it. I have a very bad feeling. I think the storms can pick times and do as they wish," said Alex.

"It isn't alive, Alex," Helen said.

"I don't know what it is. Alive. Sentient. A natural phenomenon. We don't understand, but face it, *they aren't* friendly," Alex said.

Chapter 9: Aftermath

In the morning, eating and getting camp chores done was difficult because everyone could see new things from the wrecks left by the storm on the beach. Often, they stopped to look down the beach and across the sand, wondering what the objects were. The beach was littered, and debris danced on the waves, washing in slowly.

"I can't stand it. I have to know. It may not be safe, so I'm not asking for anyone to go with me," Scott said.

"I want to go," said Benny.

"No," said Scott, giving Benny a serious, fatherly look. "I know you're mature, but you still have to learn how to fight, and we need to teach you more."

Tyrese, Alex, Scott, Stu, Davey, and Tom decided they would go. It was the most Tom had offered to do since losing his arm.

There was wreckage to explore, and on the waves, another pile of debris floated closer to the beach. In the trees, the airplane that crashed was still burning its fuel, making it impossible for anyone to have survived. As long as the wind stayed as it was, the fire wouldn't be a problem.

"I do want to see that wreckage," Alex said.

"It'll burn for days," said Benny.

"I know, but we have time. Maybe we can find out the flight; I'm curious"

The six were well armed and prepared for a fight if there were one. "Oh, shit, Scott…"said Alex as he stopped walking and talking and stared. Alex saw bodies on the sand.

"That isn't right," Stu said. He saw the bodies, too, and the strange-looking clothing perplexed him. He struggled to figure it out.

There were warped or broken boxes, long slivers of metal, a few big sections of a ship, and other debris: socks, plastic cups, a comb, wires, and equipment. There had to be at least fifty bodies on the sand. Most of them were torn and twisted into horrible shapes, with some piled high by the waves that washed them in.

"Look at that life jacket," Scott said as he pointed.

"I see it," Alex said.

"Enlighten me?" Tyrese asked. "Damn, so many dead…"

"Over three hundred, actually," Stu said quietly. "Scott, as a history teacher, you know this story, I think."

"You know how many?" Davey asked.

"I know the death count was over three hundred and that the ship was enormous, a cargo ship full of manganese ore. I know it vanished in maybe 1920, give or take a few years. I can't think straight," Stu muttered.

"1920?" asked Scott while frowning.

"Close," said Stu.

Alex rubbed his eyes. "The *Cyclops*. Yeah. Barbados. What the hell is it doing here? Holy shit. *The Cyclops*? What is it doing…"

"Same thing we are. It isn't doing anything; the ship is just *here*, like we are," said Stu, looking much paler than usual.

"But Benny is right. It doesn't fit because the shipwreck was early in the twentieth century. The plane that crashed and is still burning has to be from a later time. Does time here just jump around?" Alex asked.

"Obviously, it does," Stu said with a shrug.

"Where is the rest of the ship?" Scott asked.

Stu shrugged and said, "I bet it went straight down. I think it was close to five hundred or six hundred feet long. It was huge and full of the ore. People always wondered what caused the vanishings; it's just a storm," he said, as he laughed but wasn't smiling, and his eyes looked dark and dead.

"This island, it's just a weird anomaly. We're the ones in the wrong spot. It's just us, isn't it? We are the weird part. We don't belong," Alex suggested. His mood was still dark, and Stu's mood affected him as well. This felt wrong on so many levels, and his mind couldn't quite come to terms with what he was seeing.

Scott thought about that, gave Alex a nod, and said, "We sure aren't going home; that's for sure. Home isn't out there. We're somewhere else." The idea was as abstract as Scott had ever imagined. It was something he finally had to put into words.

He watched as other debris floated closer to camp. The waves washed the debris that direction toward the camp instead of farther down where the group was standing. The debris caught his attention, and he wondered about it, thinking that maybe it was part of *the Cyclops* that was still floating.

An odor of rot was in the air, not bad yet, but would be stronger soon. The compys would come for the bodies before anyone could bury them; there were just too many dead. This wreckage was too close to camp and might attract the larger predators, but Scott didn't know what they could do. It was too much.

"That debris doesn't look like it's from the ship, does it?" Tyrese noted as he watched some trash drift to the camp's beach.

At camp, several people walked close to the water's edge to see the debris, wondering what it was.

Tyrese didn't think it was good for them to see a bunch of bodies, but that rubbish looked different.

"It doesn't look like the ship, either. That looks like...what...trees? Bushes? Why would that be washing up?" Scott tried to see what it was. For some reason, he felt chilled even though the sun was bright, hot, and searing.

Tom and Davey started back to camp. They talked as they watched the debris; it bothered them, as well. Davey felt nervous not only because of the bodies and because of the scavengers that would come, but also because this feeling was a different kind of anxiety.

"It was a storm, so maybe parts of the island were blown out to sea by the wind and now are returning," Davey said. He had to change the topic, or he'd feel more depressed.

"That's smart. I bet you're right," Tom said.

"Those trees look funny from here. I've never seen any like those here."

"They've been tossed around; that is all."

Tyrese heard them as he caught up; he squinted and added, "No, they look funny. I have a weird feeling. Does it look wrong to anyone else?"

"Yeah, it does," Scott said. He was almost glad someone else felt the same as he did. He gave Davey a pat on the back as they walked. He and Davey never had been close friends before the wreck, but now, Scott trusted him with his life.

Stu and Alex still looked at the wreckage of *the Cyclops*.

Davey yelled, "All of you need to come on before the troodons return."

Scott chuckled.

"Oh, look, Kelly has Amanda on her feet again. I've been hoping Amanda would be okay," Davey pointed. "Tom, your mother is helping her."

"Finally. She's doing something worthwhile." Tom watched her and grimaced.

Scott and Tyrese walked past Tom and Davey and stared at their camp, seeing the debris that had landed on the shore.

Scott blinked and said, "I need glasses; I swear I saw something; what was it?" He didn't have the words. To him, the trash seemed to ripple and undulate. It wiggled. It had to be the twigs and leaves caught in the wind and water.

Tom's mother, Connie, screamed so loudly that birds in the jungle took flight, and lizards ducked under logs. She held the scream, never taking another breath, just letting it climb. Tom ran, except slower and off balance because of his missing arm, but he ran. The others ran ahead.

Alex and Stu were farther behind but moved rapidly, flying across the sand to get to camp.

Chapter 10: Death by Debris

Minutes before at the water's edge, Amanda and Connie had looked at the junk and tried to see what it was other than some branches, a few trees, enormous palm-like leaves, and bark.

Each tree was as big around as a heavy man and very tall, but few had escaped being splintered into smaller sections. Amy and her mother, Jada, went to look at the debris as well, and Jada laughed as she said that maybe a huge crate of excellent coffee had washed up. It was the first time she showed any mirth since washing ashore in her own boat wreck.

Something moved within the junk and moved without the influence of the water, and for a few seconds, the women thought maybe a survivor was there, caught in the brush. It could be that a dinosaur or a small animal was caught in the vines. Despite knowing better, Jada had a thought that it could be her husband, who was lost at sea or maybe one of the crew from their boat.

"Coffee?" asked Air Marshal Lynn, looking up, amused.

"Maybe," Jada said.

"That don't look right," Mick said. He gave Air Marshal Lynn a nod to say he'd go check it out.

"Hey, let's back away and watch to see what it is. Maybe there are critters floating along. Something is moving there," Lynn said.

"They need help," Amy said. She moved closer. "It's a survivor from one of the wrecks, maybe. He needs some help."

"No," Mick said, "don't go any closer. Something's off."

Joe was cooking a meal over the fire, but he stopped his work and stood. Along with the cooking, he was organizing and testing their supply of alcohol and deciding which tasted the best with the syrup he was cooking, as per Kelly's instructions. The mixture was something for sore throats and coughs. He was glad that one of the airplanes that crashed had been carrying large supplies to a resort.

Air Marshal Lynn began walking toward the water. He had a strange feeling, and something in Mick's voice sounded wrong. He almost felt the mood change as several people became more alert and concerned. Jada wasn't worried, but Mick's voice was different. Joe's eyes narrowed with apprehension.

Amanda almost yanked Connie off her feet as she struggled to get in front of Amy and wait for Mick.

Once she would have faced this alone, but after she was injured by dinosaur claws and then was stitched and cauterized, she needed help in case of some kind of danger.

Amanda already had seen the sinuous, slithery, sneaky movements, and as soon as she pushed in front of everyone else, the creatures, hiding among the logs and leaves, surged.

Amanda struggled to move quickly as she cried out, and her injured, scarred back felt as if it were covered in sore, leather straps. Her movements took more energy and force now since she had lost her speed and grace.

Describing the creatures was almost impossible. Each had six little 'spiderish' legs and a fat and oily, flesh-colored segmented body. Each creature was the size of a dinner plate. Little clear tails, small in comparison to their bodies, curled from their rears. The face, if that was what it was, seemed mushy and difficult to discern. There was no mouth or nose, but several pairs of black eyes sparkled and glittered. Some of the time, they rippled, skittered, and slid, instead of using their legs.

Amanda thought of ticks, slugs, and spiders.

"What are they?" Amy asked.

Amanda didn't know what they were but thought they might be prehistoric. She pushed Amy back and said, "We need to back away." She tried to push the others back, but her timing was slow.

Connie was farther away from Amanda but closest to the debris. A creature slid up Connie's ankle to her calves, enveloping them. She screamed in fear and disgust first and then with pain. Had she seen flame and smoke coming from the slug, she wouldn't have been shocked because her lower leg felt just like red-hot coals covered it.

A split second later, Amanda screamed as she felt *her* foot begin to ache and burn as if acid had been poured on her skin. She tried to stay calm, but this pain was too intense. It was worse than fire coral or anything else Amanda knew about from swimming in the ocean. Her flesh started to dissolve as she kicked at the creature.

Amanda, bending over to get the creature off her leg, had planned to scrape the mass away, but her back, covered by healing keloid scars, didn't bend, so she lost her balance and fell.

Another creature ran or slithered for her face, and when Amanda ducked, the little beast slid onto her back. Amanda let loose with whooping screams, surpassing Connie's shrieks.

Amy squealed. She realized that the creatures were attacking and she was next.

They were too close, and she wasn't brave enough to help Amanda, so she tried to back away. There was no way she could have made it to safety since two of the slugs slid and scuttled faster than she could back pedal.

Jada took one step and was suddenly between the creatures and her daughter. "Run, Amy."

Before she could follow her daughter, Jada saw that her own legs were covered by two of the fast creatures. She reached for the blobs, yanking at them, and her screams were wilder as she bucked and rolled on the beach, both of her feet and hands were covered by the secretions of the slugs.

No more than a few seconds had passed.

Mick was the closest since he had been trying to get the women to wait until they could find out what was in the debris, but he hadn't expected an attack. He was only being cautious.

He reached for the blob on Amanda's back, but it used its legs like pitons and latched on. A slimy, white ooze from its belly quickly ran over her skin like snot. The secretion dissolved her flesh, muscle, and scar tissue and then began on the bones, but with a bit more difficult.

Mick grabbed the blob, determined to break it loose, but the oozing, soft segments released more of the slime, blistering his hands at once. He jumped back, screaming with pain as the skin of his palms melted or peeled away in liquid-like strips. His flesh turned to something like melted wax and dripped to the sand.

"Acid. Oh, shit, *acid*," his voice rose as he spun in place. "*Burningggggggggg.*"

With a bat in his hands, Air Marshal Lynn ran to kill it and yelled, "Sorry, Amanda." He hit the creature still attached to Amanda. The good part was that he killed the beast.

The bad part was that as he hit the blob, it popped like a pustule of fat infection, and the stringy, oozing, clearish-white fluid flew up and covered Lynn's upper face and arms. A few spots hit his neck. Despite his strength, the pain sent him reeling. He couldn't think past the pain.

Along with the horror of the fluid covering Lynn, the creature didn't fall away from Amanda. It was dead but unable to slurp up the liquid with its series of mouths on the underside, so the ooze continued to consume her flesh.

Kelly had been using a bottle of vodka to clean a few scratches on John Littleton. As soon as the attack began, she tossed her bottle to Stu and grabbed another. She streaked across the sand, running to splash Air Marshal Lynn's face as Alex and Harold held him down on his back, yelling for someone to bring liquor.

In a time before most of the dinosaurs had evolved, these creatures lived, fed, reproduced, and died in the vegetation of the jungles. When a reptile came close, they swarmed it and fed, sucking the acid-burned flesh away from bones. They had no real intelligence, a short life span, and often starved to death. They were an old species that left no fossil records and were of little importance.

Until now.

Joe carried the left over rum from the concoction he had been testing and splashed some onto Amanda's back, as she fought to get the blob off of her back. If anyone had time to ask Joe why, he wouldn't have known why he did that, but he reacted instinctively, knowing that possibly he could set the blob on fire with the alcohol. It was all he had in his hands, and he did it without thinking.

As Joe watched, the reaction from the creature to the alcohol was unexpected but promising. The creature shriveled up to a wet husk and fell off at once. It was dead as far as he could tell.

He saw Amanda's back and was horrified by the damage, but didn't hesitate to keep trying to save his friend. He splashed her leg and killed a second slug. He yelled, "Grab the booze. Get a red-hot log, too."

It was the first time Joe had ever led a defense, and surprisingly, his voice was calm, yet it carried loudly over the screaming and made everyone pay attention. He was doing his best, and it was an excellent defensive maneuver; he only hoped people could react calmly and quickly.

Scott, Tyrese, and Davey arrived during the mayhem: hearing what Joe yelled and seeing what he did. They knew he was correct in his orders and took action at once. They reacted: Davey grabbed a smoking hot log by the unburned end, and Scott and Tyrese each grabbed a bottle of whiskey and ran faster than they had ever moved before.

Scott used half his bottle for Connie's leg; relieved that it worked as it had for Joe and Amanda. "Joe's right. Alcohol works."

Tom ran up, and with his one arm, he caught his mother as she fell. His girlfriend, Joy, ran to them. She had been on the far side of camp, and although she was terrified, she came to help.

Everything was in chaos, and Joy and Tom could hardly think, but they knew Scott had done something to help Connie.

Connie was hysterical over something real and worth being half-insane about. Both Tom and Joy felt scared for Connie as she slumped.

Scott was caught in the confusion, wondering what to do next. He was repulsed by the creatures, scared, and helpless. The group needed to fight back in an organized way, but he didn't know what else to do.

Tyrese caught another one of Kelly's bottles as she tossed it and splashed the contents on Jada's legs and chest and the slugs. She was writhing on the sand, past screaming. He felt a wave of guilt for adding to her pain, but when the creature died, he knew he had done all he could do.

"I need help, Scott," said Tyrese.

Helping to pin Jada down, Scott used the rest of his bottle to wash the stuff off of her hands, but at same time, kept himself from being covered in the goo. He did his best and was thorough, but he was petrified that Jada might grab him and get the slime on him, and then he would burn from the acid. He dodged her flailing arms but worked to save her with the alcohol.

Only Tyrese's presence kept Scott from losing his mind and running away with fear. He felt a part of a strong force that could save Jada.

"That's it," Tyrese said.

A drop of goo hit Scott's arm, and he almost screamed as a pencil eraser-sized hole burned in his arm. He steeled himself and poured the last few drops from the bottle on his arm. As bad as his pain was, considering his small wound, Scott didn't know how anyone who really was burned could still be alive. *How did anyone stand the pain of being partially engulfed? Didn't people die from sheer pain?*

"They're dead," said Tyrese.

Scott blinked and realized Tyrese meant the slugs, not the injured people.

"You okay?" Tyrese nodded to the burn Scott had suffered.

"Oh, yeah. It's nothing compared to…I'm fine. Damn, Ty. I'm glad you're here."

Tyrese's hands shook, and he shivered all over as he said, "Hell, Scott, I'm glad *you* are here. I couldn't have done it alone."

Davey poked the other creatures with the burning log, watching them shrivel and fall apart. They fell into the leaves and looked like part of the debris. He went after some more of the slugs before they attacked the people who were trying to save the wounded victims. "Burn the rest of the creatures. I have them backing off. They don't like liquor, and they don't like fire."

Joe yelled, "Burn 'em."

Mick screamed, but Davey was too busy burning other creatures. Scott and Tyrese dropped their empty bottles and grabbed the ends of burning logs to use the fire to burn the creatures, crisping them before they could attack.

There were two dozen more to kill, enough to kill each person on the beach in a most horrific manner. That idea made the men, scared of being swarmed brutally, attack the slugs.

Kelly had been using a bottle of vodka to clean a few scratches on John Littleton. As soon as the attack began, she tossed her bottle to Stu and grabbed another. She streaked across the sand, running to splash Air Marshal Lynn's face as Alex and Harold held him down on his back, yelling for someone to bring liquor.

Kelly yelled, "Hold him so the goo doesn't spread. I have this."

"We *are*. We don't want the goo flying on us," Alex yelled.

Kelly splashed, poured, and watched. The strands of goo and blobs shriveled up and stopped burning. Kelly flicked them away and used the vodka to keep cleaning, despite Lynn's screams. She had to be sure. "Thank God, it works. It really works. I'm so sorry; I know it hurts."

Stu panicked and didn't see a way to help the last victim, Mick, whose hands were burning away. He wanted to help, but Mick was still spinning and running around. In seconds, he might touch someone else with the snotty fluid and burn that person. Stu knew he had a split second to do something.

Running, Stu used all his strength and tackled Mick. Stu lay across Mick's back and held his arms straight out, hoping he was strong enough to keep Mick in place. "I need help. Come on, where's my back-up?"

Vaughn picked up a bottle and ran, taking it to Stu. While his brother, Stu, held Mick down, Vaughn poured the alcohol but had to stop several times to vomit, and the goo slid to Mick's elbows.

Stu snarled, "Get it stopped, or we're out of here, and he'll burn away. Do it right, Vaughn, or he's dead."

"Get off my ass."

"Do it right."

Vaughn braced himself and forced the nausea down. He cleaned Mick's arms just to above the elbow. Right below the elbow were bright, red and purple, bubbly burns, and lower down the arm, his wrists were nothing but bare, pitted bones. Below that where the attack had started with Mick's hands, were missing fingers, and thin, brittle sticks of yellow bones.

Stu thought Mick's screams might burst his eardrums. He second-guessed himself, wondering if he did the right thing, but he hadn't known what else to do. Yet, only a few more seconds had passed.

While Kelly worked on Lynn, John Littleton and Amy did as Kelly ordered, "Get Connie, and make sure the creatures are flicked away as husks, move her closer to the fire, and keep a check on her."

Vera stared at the sand, picked at her nails, and said, "This is too gross."

"Vera, get your ass in gear, and help Tom do the same treatment for *your* mother," Kelly yelled.

"I'm scared to touch her."

"Do it, or I'll slap you sideways, Vera."

"You wouldn't dare."

"Bet me. I said help her. Now, you idiot."

"Bitch, I...I'm trying..." said Vera, still hesitating.

"Do it. If the slugs are dead, then you're safe. I *hope*. Just *do* it."

"I am," said Vera, as she finally did as ordered, glaring at Kelly the entire time.

"Stu, get Mick settled and make sure he's okay. You did fine. All of you, there's rum or vodka or whiskey. Give them three swallows of the alcohol, and then rinse their wounds. It may ease the pain," ordered Kelly.

"Was alcohol best when we didn't know what those things were? Are? I mean..." asked Davey.

"Davey, be quiet. Yes, they need something so that they stop screaming," Kelly yelled back. She hoped she was right. She didn't wish to do harm but couldn't stand to hear the wailing of agony, but the injured people had to have relief.

Kelly couldn't imagine the pain they were experiencing. The alcohol killed the creatures, and maybe it would give the injured a measure of pain relief. Kelly needed a few minutes before she could attend to each victim of the attack.

Joe dragged Amanda back to the fireside on her belly, afraid to pick her up and cause more pain. Despite her screams again, he made her drink several gulps of whiskey and then doused her leg and back in it. He gave her four shots instead of three, thinking the amount hardly mattered. She no longer screamed when he cleaned her wounds because her vocal chords were already strained.

He asked, "Better or worse as I wash it?"

"Better," she gasped. Her eyes rolled, and she bit through her lip in several places when the pain took over her senses. Her chin became red with blood as she bit down on her bottom lip.

Joe was tender hearted, so he felt bad. Amanda was the last person from the crew of the *Connie Louise* and the person he knew best besides Durango. Not only was he lonely for the rest of the crew, but he also would be lonely for Amanda. He respected her and thought of her as a daughter.

Ever since the storm wrecked the ship, Amanda had suffered, and the suffering made Joe's heart ache. "I'd rather it be me, 'Manda. God bless but you saved Amy and tried to save everyone else today."

Vaughn, Joy, and Mattie took hot sticks and picked and poked at the edges of the debris that had washed ashore.

Harold joined Benny and Helen and helped them add anything they didn't need such as extra firewood and trash on top of the debris that Scott then set ablaze with a bottle of rum with exceptionally high proof alcohol.

To begin with, the wet trees only smoked, but the bonfire became hot as they began to add more to it, and the entire heap finally blazed. No other creatures came out, and the many that were still in the trash hiding, burned away with angry buzzing noises.

"I hope it hurts, you bastards," Harold said as he watched the fire. He wanted the creatures to suffer the keenest of misery.

Kelly called for Helen. She talked as she worked, "Marshal Lynn, take another few shots. Yeah, there you go. Five...that's good. Take a sixth. Now, relax. I'll be right back. Davey!"

"Here. I'm helping..." answered Davey.

"You help *me* now. Sit with Lynn, and keep this cloth over his face. He's safe now, but keep his face covered. Keep this hand covered as well. Wrapped. He's had enough alcohol," said Kelly as she stood with Helen. "I have to go fast, so stay with me."

"Ready," said Helen.

"That shit is some acid or something that doesn't like heat or booze. He has lost his eyes, his nose, part of his upper lip, and a spot on his chest. It isn't very deep...the place on his chest. He rubs at it, and the last three fingers on his right hand are...well...bone." Kelly didn't need to add that he was probably one of the strongest of the group and was reduced to crying like a child. She gulped as she spoke, trying to stay strong.

"He's in so much pain," said Helen.

"I know. I can't do much. It's not fair."

"Dear, God, why the hell...okay...what do we do next?" Helen asked.

"Triage, just like after the wreck. Be my second. I need Davey there," said Kelly as she went to Amanda next. Joe's eyes were wet and sad. He shook his head slowly because he had already accepted her fate.

Kelly checked Amanda's pulse and it was weak and thready. Her foot was nearly eaten away to the bone; only a little flesh and tendons remained. Her back was worse. The scar tissue was gone, along with the muscles and flesh, and her spine showed in places.

"Joe, Hon, hold her hand and keep telling her she saved the rest who were there. She was a hero because she got people away from those slugs. Tell her: 'Amanda, you did a fine job. You're amazing'."

Joe nodded. He understood Amanda was dying, and he thought that was for the best.

Jada rocked back and forth and whined with pain while Amy and Benny talked to her. Both teenagers had tears streaming down their face and were as white as paint.

Amy cried and looked up at Kelly and said, "Mom saved my life. Please fix her, Kelly. Please."

Benny was more pragmatic. "Amy, she can't work miracles." He wiped his nose on his sleeve and hugged his sister as they sobbed.

Helen and Kelly gave alcohol to Jada, but only a few shots because there was little to be done for her and alcohol would barely take the edge off any of her pain. Both felt terrible for Jada's children.

Below Jada's knees were pitted, bloody bones covered in bits of sand; no flesh was left. Because of her panic, she rubbed at her legs, covering both hands with acidic slime. Then while trying to get rid of the slime, she rubbed her hands across her shirt, covering it with the slime and causing a chest of burned areas. One breast was almost fully eaten away.

"In a little while, I could remove both her legs above the knees. She might die of blood loss and shock. Then, both of her hands will need to be removed as well. Last, I will debride her chest and breast, but all of that will be the least of her problems. I'm sorry Amy and Benny, but I have to be honest and tell you exactly what the deal is. You need to take that in. It isn't fair or right, but it's honest. Helen?"

Helen realized Kelly was asking for advice. "Both legs and both arms? You have to ask Jada," said Helen.

"We'll come back. I think...well...the shock may take her anyway," said Kelly as she turned, "and Benny, talk to Jada some and keep her calm."

"Her legs! Her hands! Kelly!" yelled Benny.

"Stop yelling at me, Benny. Do as I said, and I'll be right back. I'm sorry you have to deal with this, but who else is there? I need you. I have to check the rest, so I can't do anything yet."

"I...can't," said Benny.

"Well, yes, you can. You certainly can, and you must. Amy has to help you," said Kelly.

"It's my fault; Amanda and Mom were trying to protect me," added Benny.

"Which means you have great value. Act like it. Show that value now," Kelly said. She tightened her lips and showed a strong face even though she felt like crying.

Helen and Kelly walked away, hating to leave the teens but having to.

Kelly checked Connie who kept yelling for Durango and scratching at Tom and Vera. Her leg was in a terrible state, yet, it was one of the least severe injuries. Connie had a habit of mixing coconut oil and a little rum and then rubbing the mixture into her skin to help her tan. She had done it that morning, actually, and maybe that repelled the slug somewhat. Kelly thought about that as she checked Connie.

There were still dime-sized and nickel-sized burned holes on Connie's foot and knee, and her little toe was a tiny stump, but her leg still could be saved. "Joy, come over here, and you and Tom do what I say. Vera, go help with the fire."

"I don't wanna," said Vera.

"I said do it," Kelly snapped."Joy and Tom, use the kit, and clean the wounds well.Give Connie a few snorts of the rum. Get her very clean, and I mean wash her three times, apply cream, and then wrap her in the torn sheets after the gauze so it's cast-like."

Joy glanced at Helen who nodded that it was the right thing to do. "Is Connie okay?"

"Not okay, but she should survive this," Kelly said as she sighed. "Now for Mick."

Stu stood alone.

"Where is Mick?"

"Now, Kelly, you have to listen, okay?" said Stu.

"Where is he?" asked Kelly.

"His hands. Both are burned away to the bone, and his fingers…they're gone…it is past his wrists. The only thing to do is to remove both of his hands, Helen, and you, he, and I know that.

It's logical. That means a machete, a lot more pain, blood, fire to cauterize, and bandages, and he wouldn't have hands, Damnit."

"And?" Kelly spun, following the way Stu looked and saw Mick far out in the water. Scott, Alex, and Tyrese watched but didn't say anything. "He's going to drown?"

"He said he was swimming to China. Kind of funny. He was trying to be brave," answered Stu.

"And you let him?" Kelly asked as she yelled at Stu, almost nose to nose with him. "You stupid little shit."

"Fuck you, Kelly. It isn't always *your* choice, you know? It was his choice."

"And you are suddenly an activist for human rights? No, fuck *you*, Stu," said Kelly as her eyes burned with angry tears.

"Jada is over there, and she will lose both hands and both legs? I mean," Helen said. "Kelly, we need to go to her. Mick made his choice." She looked to Scott who returned a sad glance.

"Kelly, don't make her live that way. Let her have a choice," Stu said.

"I am. I'll give her a choice. I should have given Mick a choice, too. You had no right."

Stu leaned in close to Kelly and said, "He had a right. It isn't always about your doing shit, Kelly. I listened to him. I supported his choice. It's on me this time, like Scott always says, but it is merciful. He is in so much pain that he can't stand it another second. He is doing as he wishes."

"No, it was just easier for you, jerk. *Asshole*. Go fix the fire; stay away from me," said Kelly.

"Whatever you want."

Kelly stomped back to Jada.

Helen caught her shoulder and said, "He's a jerk, but it was Mick's decision. No one else stopped him. He lost his hands and was in excruciating pain. I can't imagine. You didn't get to decide, so? It's okay if sometimes other people decide for themselves. You aren't God, Kelly. Relax, or you're going to destroy everything."

Kelly looked to the ocean. Mick was gone, lost to the waves. "I hate losing anyone."

"Well, the hard cold fact is you're going to lose Amanda as well, and maybe Lynn and Jada as well. Buck up because we need you, and if you can't, then excuse yourself so Davey and I can do whatever is necessary. Just do something."

"Littleton! Come here, please," Kelly called. "She's your friend's wife, and the kids are sixteen and twelve and too young for this."

"For what?" asked Littleton.

"Jada is in a bad way, so come with me," said Kelly to Benny and Amy.

Kelly asked them to help with the fire. Unhappy, they walked away from their mother but relieved to be away from such suffering. Jada moaned and whined; sometimes she shrieked. Very carefully, Kelly explained the situation to Jada and John Littleton. Littleton had to be Jada's advisor.

"Both legs above the knee, and both hands? How?" Littleton asked.

"I have a few instruments, but it would be with knives and a machete, scalpels, and then hot metal…red hot…to sear the veins. Clean, cream, bandage, and hope."

"Can't bathe? Eat? Walk? A lump with a head?" Jada cried harder. "I can't take the pain; please, I can't stand it," she screamed again.

On the beach by the fire, both of Jada's children jerked as they heard her.

"I don't have anything, Jada," Kelly said.

"You'd do that surgery without putting her out?" asked Littleton as he went grey.

"I can find something to relax her a little, but put her out? No. No morphine. No drugs," said Kelly.

Jada cried with her pain and muttered that she wanted to die right then because of the pain. She frequently sobbed, "My legs!" or "My hands!" She wailed when the pain grew worse. The few swallows of vodka did little because Kelly needed her answer. If Jada passed out drunk, Kelly would remove all four limbs.

"Couldn't she pass on if she wishes?" Littleton asked. He fought to keep from vomiting.

"A scalpel to an artery, or Tyrese could probably break her neck. That would be easier on her, but not on him. You could take her out into the water and let her go; that's pretty rough though," said Helen as she tried to think. It made her sick to list the ways Jada could die. "What do you want, Jada?"

"Make it stop hurting. Oh, God, it hurts," Jada screamed again.

"If I take one limb, she'll fight for the other three and be in terrible pain, maybe worse," Kelly said.

Benny walked over and said, "Mom is a nervous person, and she has fibromyalgia. When we wrecked and went into the water, she had her purse with her watertight pill bottles in it. She has muscle relaxers, sleeping pills, nerve pills, pain pills, and something for general aches that is also a prescription. Let me sit with her, and we'll make her comfortable outside the yacht in the sand."

"Okay," said Kelly as she listened carefully.

"She can have some rum," said Benny, smiling far too widely. His eyes were shiny with shock and grief, but he kept talking, "She can have...oh, a few of each pill or several, and any that are left, you can have for your medical kit, Kelly. If there are any left. Amy and I can sit with her, and we'll help the pain until it all goes away."

"My, God," Kelly said.

Helen blinked away tears and said, "It's the best idea we have, Kelly. We'll get her moved and all comfy. Benny," she couldn't continue.

"You're brave," Kelly said.

"No. I'm a coward. I can't stand hearing her suffer."

Benny helped, and they took Jada, wrapped in her sheets, outside so she could see the waves while she lay in a little depression in the sand.

Benny gave her the rum mixed with fruit juice; next, he gave her pain pills and finally sleeping pills, adding more to his palm as he counted them out.

After a few pain pills and sleeping pills and the rum, Jada quieted, talking dreamily to her children and letting them comb through her hair and pat her face and shoulders. They kissed her, and she smiled at Amy and Benny. Kelly and Helen cried as they watched.

The only unusual event happened when Jada asked for Helen, right as Jada began with the second round of pills. She was relieved of some of the pain but still able to focus. "Helen, Benny adores you. You'll take my babies, and make sure they're safe?"

"Amy and Benny?"

"Please?"

Helen cried openly, "Oh, Jada. I'll treat them like my own children if you want. If they want."

Jada smiled peacefully and said, "Benny, Amy, your father and I, will watch over you, but here, Helen will care for you. You mind her; be safe and good, okay?" Her eyes rolled as the pain hit her in waves.

Amy pressed her face against her mother's face and wept as she nodded. Benny patted Amy and looked at Helen. "Sorry, it's the only thing we can do. It's my mother; she has to arrange something she is good with," he whispered. "Just agree. It won't matter because she won't know anyway. It's more peaceful for her."

"I'm giving my word. I'll care for you and Amy as my own," Helen promised. "Goodbye, Jada."

Helen left the children with their mother, walked a few steps, and buried her face in her hands as she cried.

Chapter 11: Nothing in Common

Joe asked some others to help him, and they carefully and respectfully added Amanda's body to the bonfire so that no creatures would dig her up and eat her.

Her sheet-covered body settled deep in the blaze and burned away.

"She was a hero. She saved Amy and probably Connie as well. Bad times. I gotta boil water and cook rice. Don't mind me," said Joe.

"I'll help you," Davey offered to Joe. He needed to walk away from death for a while. Besides, Joe needed someone to talk to.

"I caused her pain when I moved her, Davey. I didn't mean to."

"Joe, you tried to save her and the others. If you hadn't done it, we might all have died. She didn't blame you for that. She knew you stopped the creatures from burning her more. It was just too late."

Joe wiped his eyes.

"You tried. We can't do more than try," said Davey.

"I miss her already. She was a strong lady," Joe said, remembering Amanda and him working together aboard the *Connie Louise*.

Davey patted Joe's arms and nodded. "I liked her a lot."

At lunch, the group picked at the fruit and smoked meat because each had very little appetite. Everyone looked depressed, so there was little conversation. Benny and Amy, with Littleton's help, wound Jada's body tightly and allowed Scott, Alex, and Tyrese to put her corpse in the bonfire, too. Littleton held the hands of the children, they prayed a while, and then they cried.

Littleton walked over to Helen and said, "They're your children now, but I don't know why she didn't trust them to me."

"John, it must have been because I've been here longer and she wanted a mother-type, a female." Helen was guessing. His words made her feel uncomfortable.

"Or, maybe we'll end up married, and they can be *our* children," Littleton said as he looked at Helen and then walked away.

"What the hell?" Scott asked.

"He's in shock, Scott. I don't see me marrying him, not when I have you. We're all mentally messed up right now," Helen said, "and he's not in his right mind anyway." She gave Scott a kiss before going to sit with Benny and Amy.

Scott nodded. He really didn't see Helen with Littleton, and he hoped Littleton understood that. It was strange for another man to say such a thing to Helen. He watched Helen with Amy and Benny. Then, Vera walked by them, nose pointed upwards. Scott thought she was a strange, selfish girl.

"Vera, do you want to join us? Amy is your age?" asked Helen as she beckoned to the girl. "Come talk to us."

The pet dinosaur-bird was perched on Vera's shoulder, preening; his green and yellow feathers were beautiful and bright in the drab surroundings.

Vera wrinkled her nose and said, "My mom won't stop complaining, so Tom and Joy can deal with that, but I don't think I'll join in…"

"Why not? You can talk to Benny and Amy," said Helen.

Vera sneered and said, "I doubt we have much in common."

"You might," Helen said, "why not see if you do?"

"What do you mean?" Amy asked. "We have nothing in common? So?"

Vera looked at Amy and asked, "Were *you* a cheerleader? Were *you* voted most popular? Was *your* room decorated like a princess's bedroom? Was it pink, shiny, and unbelievably expensive? Did *you* have *all* designer clothing and never had to wear the same thing twice? Did people *beg* to do *your* homework for you so you'd be nice to them? Did *your* father *own* the yacht you were on?"

Each time a question was asked, Amy shook her head, no.

"That's what I meant. Nothing in common."

"I didn't need all that. I was a majorette, though," said Amy.

"So, band geek?" replied Vera.

"Snob," Amy muttered.

"Bitch," Vera snapped back.

"She's pretty, though," said Benny, defending his sister. "In fact, Vera, she's prettier than you. Leave her alone. You're being a jerk."

"Whatever, but we have zero in common, and she is not prettier. She's ugly."

Helen bristled and said, "Vera, you have none of those things now. They are all gone, but both of you have lost fathers, so that's a commonality. Why are you being mean to Amy? She just lost her mother."

"And? There's nothing anyone can do. I'm going to teach Angus new tricks. That's more interesting. Really, I have nothing to add to this group," said Vera.

"I agree. You really have nothing to add," Helen said.

Amy sniffed back tears again.

"She's a little meanie," Helen caught herself. "Thank you for the pills, Benny. Both Connie and Air Marshal Lynn are in less pain and are sleeping."

"Glad to help. How long has Vera had that little dinosaur?" Benny asked.

"The bird? Angus?"

"It's a dinosaur. Really. A young one."

"A few days. Why?" Helen wondered.

"I don't know; it reminds me of something…a type of, but I can't think right now. My head aches from crying."

Helen showed Benny and Amy two pills. "One for each of you. You need some long, healing sleep. Let's get you tucked in."

Neither complained that it was barely after noon, and both fell asleep in the yacht. Helen tucked them in and steeled herself to keep from slapping Vera. How anyone could be so cruel was beyond her imagination.

Helen sat with the others who ringed the fire pit, faces tired and strained.

Chapter 12: Specimen Bank

As dusk fell, the compys came in large packs to feed on the poor dead sailors who had washed up on the beach. A few troodons lumbered down and ate most of the bodies, cracking the bones, staying away from the survivors. The bonfire kept them away and served to shelter everyone's view of the carnage.

By the morning, most of the bodies were either gone, or the bones were cleaned and scattered, and the predators left before dawn.

As the humans sat around the fires, Helen dared to ask, "Okay, I saw the creatures and what they did. I know how they kill; I mean I get it was like acid. Can someone tell me what those slug-creatures were? Where they came from? I've never heard of anything like those."

"Did you ever read Lovecraft?" Davey asked.

"No, should I have?"

Davey shrugged.

"They aren't like that, Davey. I don't know the name, and neither does Benny because I asked. They are some kind of slugs...blobs... invertebrates and the trees, very old..."Alex said. "I think those were among the first creatures on earth. Very old. I get the Lovecraft reference, Davey. Very cool, but wrong. They're just weird, old animals."

"They're scary," Helen said.

Alex agreed and said, "Maybe long ago, the storms brought the dinosaurs, maybe two by two and put them here. The storms last night brought a ship from the early twentieth century, an airplane from the twenty-first century, and slugs from the past. The storm collects. Maybe it'll bring weird shit from the future."

"Meaning?" Davey asked.

Alex sighed and said, "Meaning we are a large specimen bank. Or we are on Noah's Ark. Or we are something else, but one day, what if a storm brings even worse things from long ago?"

"Worse than slugs?" Scott asked. He came over and sat so that he could hold Helen tightly.

She shivered and asked, "Worse than dinosaurs?"

"Oh, sure. Maybe it's mythology, or maybe it's when people wrote about giants, old demons, and things that terrified ancient people, the things of nightmares and legends. I don't know."

"You're drunk," Stu said.

Alex grinned and answered, "Yup, 'cause I am scared to death of this place. I told you that the storm collects. One day it may collect something far worse…"

Chapter 13: Healing

More than a full week, but closer to two weeks, the survivors experienced a variety of emotions, and the only good thing that could be said was that without television, telephones, and other distractions, they were forced to deal with reality much faster than was usual. With no escapism, they faced their personal mourning and stayed busy with physical activities. Tyrese half-joked that they were sweating away their grief.

There was no way for Benny or Amy to escape from thinking about losing their mother, so they talked about their feelings, sharing the same sadness. They recalled funny things and difficult times about growing up, compared what they loved most about Jada and what drove them mad about her; in fact, they actually talked and listened.

Both agreed that Jada had been enormously brave when she stepped between the slug and Amy to save her daughter, acting selflessly and lovingly. They discussed how Jada's last moments of clarity centered on making sure a responsible, smart, and, most important, loving adult would watch over them.

Helen.

Jada's consideration gave Benny and Amy some peace, knowing her love was so strong that she thought of what was best for her children right up to the end, despite her own terror and pain.

Benny and Amy were sharp enough to understand that they weren't quite old enough to make their own choices in wise ways and had only to look at Vera to see how young people could go so wrong. Jada was intelligent enough to know Helen would take the role seriously.

Mattie and Harold took the deaths of Air Marshal Lynn and Mick the hardest, but actually, everyone was fond of Lynn and missed his strength around camp. His dependability and levelheaded choices always made everyone feel a little safer. Sadness was shared, and everyone having lost the strong, brave man, Lynn, seemed a little surreal.

Tom and Joy left Connie only when Stu and Vaughn sat with her, so all of them helped rub soothing creams and oils into the wounds after cleaning the flesh, and then they gently wrapped her leg as Kelly directed them. Connie wasn't healed, but she was slowly getting better. She complained often, which Tom jokingly said was a positive sign that she would be all right.

Joe cooked little more than plain rice, beans, and fish, food he didn't even bother to season very well. Breakfast was fruit or smoked meat, and lunch was whatever he dumped in his largest pot: meat or fish, shellfish, and random vegetables. He continued to stare out to sea with big, wet eyes. He wasn't over Durango, and he missed Amanda fiercely.

Three light storms brought nothing new to the beach, but luckily, didn't come with the dreaded yellowish cast to the sky and waves. The storms did add to the group's supply of rainwater even though the group was able to go to the closest spring for drinking water, so fresh water wasn't a problem.

Positive time in camp was spent improving weapons and making the yacht more comfortable, yet, everyone complained about the rainstorms.

Helen spent more time with Amy and Benny, finding them both to be wonderful wards, whom she was now responsible for. They accepted her as easily as she did them. Scott noticed she took to being a surrogate mother easily, and his only concern was that John Littleton always found excuses to work alongside Helen.

On the third day after the initial attack, the group gave Air Marshal Lynn a burial at sea, allowing his weighted and wrapped body to sink deep in the water. As Scott helped, he felt even more guilt, and he knew he was beginning to take each loss as a personal affront.

Chapter 14: Big Brown Returns

The jungle was unusually calm, which made a few of the survivors nervous, but there were no snorts or roars to alert them to a hunting pack. Other than the compys and troodons that cleaned the beach of bodies, which unfortunately continued to wash inland from the wrecked the *Cyclops*, no one saw any wildlife.

They remembered Big Brown had been absent from the beach for a long time. He was large, mostly brown, but lightly covered in feathers that ended with bright blue tip plumage that helped his species attract mates. He had a mate that was big with babies, but she had attacked the camp and had been killed.

While he didn't retain exact memories, he did feel drawn to the beach and could still find traces of the female's scent at times, which faded with each storm.

Her scent was still one of anger, pain, and misery, and because he no longer saw her at the beach, he felt the same. Those were not emotions as humans might have, just scents that manifested with aggression.

He was also careful at the beach because he did feel it was dangerous to him; his instincts warned him to stay away, despite being drawn back.

On the fourteenth day after the slug attack, Big Brown made an appearance. His weight caused loud thuds as he ran and roared.

Big Brown ran past the tree line and would have kept going, but paused as he recognized that other creatures were making noises and coming toward him. He wasn't concerned about attacking a few of the smaller creatures, and he would have eaten them gladly, but he had learned to avoid a large pack of the humans, the same way he avoided packs of any predators.

The human that Big Brown had been chasing kept running until she was past the people who were armed for a fight, knowing that she was safer with the group than she would be with the big dinosaur. She fell right at Kelly's feet and became dizzy, as Tyrese lifted her and carried her to safety.

Davey and Scott advanced on Big Brown with their spears and ducked his gaping maw of sharp teeth as they stabbed at him. Davey blinked away the steam of hot, salty blood that flew at him, as Big Brown dodged and swung his body around to retreat.

"Die, damnit," yelled Scott, as tried to hit the beast with his spear but lost his aim when he jumped to the side. Big Brown's tail almost knocked Scott off his feet.

Before they could try again, Big Brown lumbered off with a roar, leaving the humans alone and frustrated on the beach. While they might not have wanted or been prepared for a large fight, having Big Brown run away meant that the fight was only delayed; he was a reoccurring threat.

The rest were armed now and were ready to fight, but then they saw the dinosaur leave. They shrugged at Scott and Davey.

"Good aim," Scott said.

"Thanks. All it or I did was scratch him," said Davey.

"Enough that you'll have to wash up. He's lucky we weren't more prepared."

"We were prepared enough to drive him away and save that girl. I wonder who she is?"

Scott waited for Davey to clean himself in the ocean, watched for Big Brown, and walked back to camp to find out whom they had saved.

Mattie and Harold were animated, talking more and gesturing as Scott and Davey joined the rest. Kelly washed the girl's cuts and scrapes and muttered to Helen as she did. Kelly looked up and then went back to her work.

"Who is that?" asked Helen.

Stu frowned and said, "We don't know everything yet. Mattie and Harold know her and say that her name is Cindy. She was on their plane and went away with the other children when that group broke away and went out to live in caves."

Mattie nodded, "She was with Jody, Ricky, and the rest, the last we knew. She was a pretty little girl. A sweet little thing."

Scott was flummoxed. It seemed to him that they were discussing two different people. The wounded girl was really a woman, skinny, mottled with bruises, and covered with bleeding cuts. She was wearing rags for clothing: a crude vest made of matted fur and foot coverings of leather that were barely shaped into short boots.

Her dirty hair was hacked off below her ears, and might have been sandy-colored or blonde if clean. Her exposed stomach was bloated with a few months of pregnancy that made her look more starved than healthy.

"A kid," Scott asked, "but she isn't a little girl, Mattie."

Mattie sighed and said, "She was. That steroid water they drank caused them to reach puberty quickly. She was a child, and then she looked eighteen or twenty, but she was still pretty, then."

"She looks like she's in her late twenties," said Scott.

"She's aged badly," Mattie said.

"She's coming around. Don't interrogate her. She's not doing very well," Kelly warned. "Cindy? You're safe here."

"Do you remember me?" Mattie said as she knelt. She tried to smile, but it came as a grimace.

Cindy blinked and ran her tongue over her dry lips and took a sip of water from Kelly as she watched everyone suspiciously. "Yeah, Mattie?"

"What happened to you out there? Were you alone?" Scott asked.

"Alone. Yeah. Then that thing come after me, and we fought in the jungle. He mushed me; I hurt."

Kelly told her, "You're injured pretty badly. I have no idea how you were running because I think you have several broken bones, and you have some deep cuts."

"Scared. I just ran."

"Adrenaline," Kelly said.

"Were you alone?" Mattie needed answers.

"Yeah, I said I was. I wasn't before. He done trashed our camp."

"Did he kill the rest of your murdering friends?" Stu demanded. He had come up to see the young woman and hated her as he hated all of the feral children. They had killed a woman he really liked, or that he enjoyed having sex with. Same thing.

"Hey, back off a little," Scott ordered. He understood why Stu hated the group of kids Cindy was with, because they had almost killed Stu and did kill the woman he was with. The leader of the group was Mattie's son. They had various views of the group, but Stu wasn't going to get answers by saying what Mattie's son did in a demanding way. "Were you with the other kids?"

"Yeah. We was down that way on the beach…long way from here, and that big brown thing come after us. He killed a bunch, and we never seen him coming. We wasn't paying attention."

"Is Jody dead?" Mattie asked.

"I hope he is," Stu answered.

Scott held up a hand. "Shhh. Can it, Stu."

Tyrese moved closer, worried that Stu might harm Cindy.

"I don't know. They ran. Ran! They left us there. Bastards."

"Yeah, they are," Stu grinned, "all bastards."

"Stop it," Scott demanded.

"Oh," Mattie breathed a small sigh of relief.

"Awe, come on…" Stu was irritated, and if he were in charge, he would like to take the girl and feed her to the dino. She was from a group of cannibal kids and was useless. He hadn't forgotten the beating he got from a few of the bastard children.

"Stu, it's Mattie's son. Ease off. We need fewer emotions here and more information," said Kelly as she begged for peace with her eyes. She was one of the few people Stu listened to. After their fight the day of the slug attack, they had made up, becoming more affectionate and even sleeping together.

Tom never said a word about his former fiancée, Kelly, or his brother Stu, but he didn't approve and showed it.

"They runned off like cowards. A few of us had to run the other way," Cindy said.

"And where are *they*?" Scott asked Cindy.

"Troos."

"True?" Scott asked.

"Trudys."

"Troodons," Alex joined in, "and did they attack you?"

"Uh-huh. Juan, Carla, Dante, and Colt, and the brown one. Days and nights. He followed us. I hurt." Cindy moaned and rubbed at the cuts and held her stomach, gasping. She was starting to show new bruises in smudged patches all over her skin.

"She's been on the run for days. These older cuts are from something smaller than Big Brown. I think they're from the troodons. She has a lot of infection from cuts. She's very, very sick," Kelly said.

"Brown got me, not long ago."

Kelly nodded. That made sense. Big Brown scattered the camp that Cindy had been a part of, but the troodons were the ones that injured her so badly. It had to have been days before since Cindy had fought them, and Kelly wondered how a lone woman was able to get away from them. Big Brown had followed Cindy, maybe, but he was also patrolling his territory, and he had caught her not far from the beach.

"Why didn't we hear anything?" Scott asked. It was exactly what Kelly had been about to ask.

"He mushed me. I done told you that."

"You let him get that close? You didn't scream? We didn't hear him roaring like he does when he attacks."

"He stepped on me and tried to kill me, okay. I was sneaking here," said Cindy as she groaned again. "I was lying on my belly and watching you."

"I knew it. She's no better than the rest. She was spying," Stu said, pointing at her and condemning her.

"Spying on what, Stu? On how we fish? On what we're doing for chores? What is she spying on? Nothing. She was watching us. Right?"

"Whatever you think," Stu said. He rolled his eyes and made a face.

"Were you coming here for help?" Scott asked as he turned back to Cindy.

"Yeah, look, they ain't right: Jody and Ricky. They eat the dead, and that ain't right."

"You want them to eat people who are alive?" Alex asked.

"Idiot. No. Us. If one of us done dies, they eat *us*. They don't care. They just eat us up even though they know us. That's sick shit," said Cindy as she groaned with pain.

"Well, welcome to how your type works, bitch. You didn't care when it was *you* eating other people, huh? And raping and torturing?" Stu exploded.

Scott didn't say anything. Stu was right about that. He conceded that.

"Did you know your people raped and killed Lori?" Kelly asked.

Cindy turned her face away from Stu but faced Kelly and said, "I didn't do that. They did it. I wasn't there."

"Maybe you weren't, but they did it. Have you and your group eaten other people?" Scott asked. "That's hard for us to accept...cannibalism. It's sick and cruel; do you get how we feel?"

Cindy spoke to Kelly instead. "We had to. There ain't always other things, and the dinos eat us. It all comes around. Jody said it."

"He did not. Jody was always a good person. He is good hearted. That water made all of you this way," Mattie said.

"Water didn't make them anyway, Mattie. They still had choices, and Cindy, we don't eat people, and yet, we do fine. That's no excuse," Scott tried to appease everyone.

"We're just trying to survive. That made us whatever way you think we are. It ain't the water, I guess. It's Jody. He's crazy. He don't care. Says we are meat, and sooner or later we all get eaten, so it may as well be us doing the eating."

"How can you blame him for everything? Didn't you have a voice?" Mattie was getting more upset.

"Sick bitch. Why're we wasting time here? We should feed her to Big Brown," Stu said.

Cindy's eyes went large as she begged, "Don't feed me to him. Is he your pet or something? You control them dinosaurs?"

Vera walked closer and had her pet dinosaur Angus on her shoulder. She stared at Cindy and acted as if she smelled something bad as she curled her upper lip and wrinkled her nose.

Stu used the opportunity. "Maybe we do. I want to know where your camp is, and I want to know if Jody and the rest are alive."

Cindy pointed. "That ways. I don't care anyway. I wanted to get away from them before they ate me. I'm glad all that happened with us scattering."

Mattie pulled away as if she had been slapped and said, "That is *not* like my son."

Scott looked at her calmly, "Mattie, Jody has been on his own a while, and the water sure as hell made the kids aggressive. He may have changed since you were around him. It sounds like he's become feral."

"And? He's either killing people, or he's dead and has been left out there in the jungle to rot. I have to find my son," said Mattie as she shook her head. "This is horrible, but if he is alive, I have to talk to him."

"You want him? Find him. I never wanna see those bastards again. They'll eat me," Cindy said.

Kelly checked Cindy's fever again and wiped away infection that blossomed around a cut on the girl's belly. "Because of the baby? Did you think you were going to die giving birth?"

"It hurt."

"I know. Cindy, you had contractions and panicked, didn't you? Was that why everyone was distracted? Then Big Brown came and then the troodons, and you ran to us."

"Whose baby is it?" Stu asked.

Cindy rolled her eyes, "Who cares? It didn't come out. I don't care anymore."

"The baby isn't moving. I think you know that. Her fever is going up," said Kelly as she gave them a glance and felt of Cindy's forehead.

"I'm sick," said Cindy.

"I know. You can sleep and rest here, though. No one here will hurt you. You have to rest, and everyone can calm down," Kelly said.

Cindy gripped Kelly's hand, "But you won't eat me?"

Scott felt sick, too. "No matter what you've done and who you were with before, it doesn't matter. We won't eat you. Nothing will eat you, I promise."

"I'm sorry," said Cindy as she looked at Mattie and relaxed. "He ain't right. Don't go looking for him, Mattie. He'll just hurt you if you go searching. Jody changed. He's mean now."

Mattie didn't answer. She tightened her lips and wiped her eyes. No matter what Cindy said, Mattie wanted to see her son. She loved him. "I can't accept that he isn't still the son I know. There's more to this…"

Disgusted, Stu walked away, and some of the rest watched Cindy, curious but afraid to ask anything more. Kelly said the girl wasn't doing well and shouldn't be questioned.

Away from her patient, Kelly explained that Cindy had been moving on pure adrenaline, trying to find a safe place to die; she somehow knew she wasn't going to survive her injuries. "I think the fever began because the baby died and she didn't deliver it. I don't know if the injuries and infections were serious enough to kill her before, but I suspect they were. That is second. Big Brown broke some bones, and that is the third problem."

"She should be dead three times over is what you mean?" Helen asked.

"Yes, she isn't going to survive this," said Kelly as she took deep breaths. It was the first time she had stopped fighting death, and it was new to her. She knew there was nothing she could do, and she had to admit it. "Maybe I can deal with the baby and the infection, but I can't do much for the broken bones inside of her. They're causing bleeding internally."

"How is she alive and conscious?" Helen asked.

"Like I said, she's running on adrenaline, but her body is being overwhelmed quickly. She wasn't well fed or healthy before, and it's catching up with her too rapidly to repair. She's got too many strikes against her, honestly, and I can't do much about this."

"Then, you can't. We understand that, Kelly," Scott told her.

Cindy died by dawn, and as Scott had promised, they wrapped her and let her go into the ocean so that nothing would eat her. Stu made several comments about letting Big Brown have her, but he didn't push his ideas.

Mattie paced the camp and frequently told Scott that sooner or later, they would have to go in search of her son and find him dead or find him alive and face him. She said they had to know if Jody were alive, and if so, *she* had to know what was going on in his mind.

They went back to daily chores and waited for Big Brown to attack again, but he stayed away, and everyone teased Davey about scaring the big dinosaur away from the beach. Davey carried his lucky spear wherever he went.

"You're like a caged animal," Helen said. The day after Cindy died, Helen watched Scott walking around camp aimlessly, stopping and staring into nothing and then walking again. He often whispered with Mattie and Harold, sometimes with Alex, and a few times, he and Tom walked together.

Scott shrugged and said, "I hate mysteries. I know there are no answers, but I still want to know what's out there."

"Dinosaurs."

"I know that, smarty pants," Scott winked at Benny.

"Snakes. Slugs."

"Right. I seem to remember those as well," said Scott.

Helen was amused, "Then, what is it you are looking for?"

"I have no idea. I guess I will know it if I find it. I want to know more about the airplane that crashed, who might be on the island with us, and what goes on over on the other side. We don't even know how big this place is." He paused. "I'd like to know if Mattie's son and that group are still a danger or if they're dead."

"As for the size of the island, I can say one thing: it's huge if it supports the creatures we've seen. Alex agrees," Benny said.

"Every time anyone goes exploring, we lose people," Helen reminded them.

"That's why I'm going with only a few people. Wait, before you get angry, the kids need you, Helen. I'll be fine and can move faster and easier with only a few people. That leaves more here to defend the camp."

Helen's eyes narrowed. He had obviously already planned his trip to explore the island and hadn't told her until now. She understood his reasoning, but that didn't make her any less afraid. "When are you going?"

"In a few minutes. I didn't want to fight over this."

"Wow. Okay. There isn't much I can say," said Helen.

"I have to know these things about this place. I need it. We have to know more if we expect to survive," Scott said.

"Come home safely is all I ask," said Helen, as she tried to talk around the lump that filled her throat.

She felt sick as she watched him walk away with the worst possible group: Alex who was increasingly afraid of his own shadow, Tom who had only one arm to fight with, and Mattie, who was bitter, but desperate to find her son. Harold was a good worker but a poor fighter, and the sixth member of the team was Joy, Tom's girlfriend, who followed him blindly. Helen noticed that Kelly looked at Tom and Joy with sad eyes.

"I tried to talk sense into Scott," Tyrese told Helen.

"It's the way he thinks; he's too curious for his own good, and I don't think he feels it'll work out very well for him."

"He doesn't?" said Tyrese.

"No, he took the people we can stand to lose, those who are worn out and tired. He doesn't expect the search to go well. He can't risk you or me this time, Ty," said Helen as she turned away and refused to watch Scott and the other five walk into the jungle. She knew they wouldn't be returning.

Chapter 15: Into the Unknown

Scott felt the odds were about fifty-one percent that he would be the cause of Helen's death, and if he watched her die, he'd probably kill everyone else before drowning himself. That wasn't good. On the other hand, he thought he might save her life, but gave that only a forty-nine percent probability. In asking Alex, one of the smartest men he knew, Scott was attempting to get another opinion on his musings.

"I think it's more even, really, but that doesn't say much either, because you might save us, or cause us to get killed, right? I'm not sure I like knowing my odds are half or less at surviving this trip or any trip with you," replied Alex.

"You've got it all wrong. We had a lot with us when we met you people, and we are now down to two. I'm not a whiz at math, but isn't that poor odds?" Mattie asked.

"I wasn't to blame for Lynn or Lori or the others," said Alex.

"We could debate that. I'm just trying to help," Mattie said. "I know if you run into my kid, I'm all that may keep you alive. Besides, maybe we can bring them around and help them. I want my son back. I'm going to find Jody."

"I'm going because of Mattie. Who else does she have except me?" Harold asked.

"Your son may attack us. Mattie, you probably won't be able get through to him," Scott said.

"I can try. At least I'll have that: I tried."

"I can't deal with my mother's constant suffering and Stu's bossiness and Vera's bitchiness right now," Tom said as he readied himself to go, "and I'm tired of seeing the smug look Kelly wears all the time. She's sleeping with Stu now."

"Slut," Joy said.

Alex snorted, remembering how Joy had slept her own way around the campfire, but he didn't bring it up, saying only, "Scott may need me to identify a dino."

"Littleton moons over Helen. What about him?" Mattie asked Scott.

"She can handle him. Maybe they belong together, but I doubt he's her type." As he turned to Tom, Scott told him, "Kelly is a good person, and you can't keep holding a grudge."

"Sure I can. I tried to forgive her, but I can't. It isn't just that she hacked off my arm because I get that: she did it to save me, but it's more than that. I can't wrap my mind around the fact that she betrayed me when she made the choice, but then she didn't stand by it."

"Huh?" Alex asked.

"She makes excuses and wants me to understand. If from the get-go, she had just said that she was the expert and made the decision, I could have dealt with it. She backtracked it and won't own up to it. Same with Stu. She hated him and feared him a little maybe, and then she sleeps with him. Why?"

"She wants sex?" Alex laughed.

Tom smiled but shook his head and said, "No, she sleeps with him because she won't stand up to him and own her actions. She does it to placate him. Same as she does me."

Scott frowned. "Maybe she's scared, Tom. You're being a little rough on her."

"Yeah?"

"I mean you fooled around with Joy first. You cheated on Kelly before she ever cut off your arm."

"I remember it well. As soon as we got back, I was sick, almost crazy with infection, and you don't know this, but I told her that I was afraid I was dying and wanted to come clean. Thing is, I didn't die, did I? Hell hath no fury, Scott."

"Oh hell, Tom! There is no way she did that as revenge."

Tom shrugged at Scott and said, "Whatever you think, but I'm telling you, she did, and I'm also telling you that she and Stu are snakes of a feather."

"Snakes don't have feathers," Joy said.

"Dinosaurs do, though," Alex said.

They walked past the giant bones that were left in a pile on the beach, the ones that Alex and Benny had been so interested in. Alex took less interest and didn't look at them except once as they passed by. With no one to talk to about them, they were less interesting.

They made camp on the beach two nights in a row, hoping the fire would keep them safe. They fished and ate some of the food they brought and found a large supply of coconuts for their water.

The empty coconuts shells caught the water from a short but plentiful rain shower the second evening and allowed the group to refill their bottles and canteens. More coconuts went onto the small sled they pulled. They carried extra food, a few tarps, blankets, cooking utensils, and more weapons on the little sled as well.

"That's unusual," Harold said, wiping his face. He stopped to look at boulders that stretched out into the ocean in one direction, as far into the jungle as he could see in the other direction. "Forty? Fifty feet tall?"

"I told you I was beginning to believe in giants," Alex snickered. He led them up and down the boulders that they found first. "Look, we can suck in our guts and maybe get through that part there; see the shady area?"

"Why?" Joy frowned.

"Why not? That's what we're here to see, Joy, to find out what is in all the places we've never seen." Tom took the lead and wiggled between two of the boulders, kicking sand, rubbing away loose dust, and pushing along.

The crack was only ten feet long, the width of the giant boulders, but Tom was scraped and scratched before he made it through. "Go slowly, Joy, suck it in, and raise yourself up to find wide places, and then go lower when you need to. Plan your moves."

"I'm stuck!"

"Of course, you would be, Joy," Scott muttered. He wasn't very surprised to hear her calling for help.

Scott sighed and climbed into the crack behind Joy and pushed and poked her until she popped out the other side; she bled from scrapes and cursed.

Alex had to do the same for Harold who was stuck for several minutes, until Alex helped him dig a lower space in the sand so that Harold could drop lower and crawl through. Tom yanked at Harold with one arm.

Thin and small, Mattie made it through with ease. She grinned and showed off that she hadn't even scratched herself while crawling through the boulders. She brushed sand off her legs.

Joy had already forgotten her cuts and bruises as she ran from spot to spot, squealing. "Oh my, God. Do you see all of this?"

"Is that an avocado, and pears? Figs. It's a garden of fruits," said Scott as he cheered happily. "You have to be kidding me. Did we hit the Garden of Eden? Figs! I have died and gone to Heaven."

"Oh, that? Yeah, there is a variety of fruit, but it gets better. Growing over there is kale, and those are fiddlehead ferns; they are delicious, and there are nuts and root vegetables," said Alex.

"Why?" Scott asked Alex.

Alex looked around and smiled, "Someone made a garden, cultivating it and making sure good food grew here. I mean nutritious but good-tasting food. It's gone wild now, but it's all edible." It was a perfect spot because only the compys could get inside of the walled garden.

"Giants didn't build it?" Scott teased. He popped berries into his mouth and peeled an orange. "How is it there are walls made of boulders?"

"I doubt it was a giant. I still have hope, but no, someone normal built it, I guess. Who knows? It looks like from the size of these trees that someone planted them to grow here long ago. Maybe fifty or more years ago? Longer probably," said Alex as he laughed crazily at all the fresh food.

"Someone built a walled garden? Does this make sense?" Scott asked.

"Not in the least," Tom said as he ate an avocado, relishing the soft flesh of the fruit.

"Everything makes some sense once you get all the information. People once thought dinosaurs were giants. They were, and we learned they lived on earth, and then, I started to say *died off*. I guess they didn't go extinct in some places or even in all times. We don't understand that, but understanding doesn't make anything more or less real," Alex said.

"You're so brainy," Joy said. "You always did like reading and studying, but I had fun in college."

Mattie rolled her eyes and said, "Which is more helpful now? Knowledge or that fun you had?"

"Mattie..." Tom began.

Alex interrupted, "Tell you what, Tom, you get me some fish, shellfish, and shrimp, and I'll make camp and cook you a dinner that Joe would be shamed by. Trust me. Leave Joy to help me. We'll make Joe green with envy when we tell him."

Tom laughed and said, "Okay. Deal. *You* can tell Joe and get him pissed off, but *I* won't complain a bit over this."

For the next few hours, they brought back food: fish, shellfish, and an unlucky trio of compys. Alex and Joy picked, cleaned, and cooked dinner.

With a big grin, Alex served shrimp cooked with coconut over something odd that he told them was quinoa.

"I've never heard of quinoa," Mattie said.

Alex was pleased to find he could teach them about it, explaining it was common in South America and very unremarkable. He told them, "It's good because it's new to you, and you can cook it as a porridge, too. Breakfast."

There was a salad of palms, raw kale, cashews, and lemongrass that was dressed with fresh orange juice and shallots. Alex enjoyed having to explain what each dish was, and while each contained ordinary foods, having so much food and of such a fresh variety was a rare occurrence for the survivors

"Kale?" Scott frowned, "Isn't that a health food? I don't know about health foods..."

Mattie smiled and said, "You may not know about them, but you sure did eat a lot of salad. Hey, it's good for you, but it doesn't mean it isn't good in general. I always told my son that."

Scott nodded. He didn't want Mattie to become depressed again. "Don't tell Joe, but this is great." He tried to get back on topic.

"It's a breeze to cook, too," Joy said.

She served several fish that were stuffed with hot peppers, oysters, fennel, and garlic and served with taro roots, somewhat like potatoes.

"This was easy to make. It's only fancy because we don't have all this back at the *Connie Louise*."

When everyone was full, Alex produced an ugly, stinky melon that all of them recoiled from. He laughed and cut it open and talked them into trying bites. "Trust me," he said. Even though it smelled terrible, the taste was fresh, sweet *and* tart, and creamy. It was delicious, and Alex said it was a durian melon.

"Amazing," Scott said as he ate a piece of the melon.

"We could have cooked four or five times this much in combinations with other things we found that we didn't even use. I also found ginger root," said Alex.

"You have to be kidding," Tom told Alex.

"Nope. It's literally an old garden of nuts, herbs, trees, fruits, and vegetables. Breakfast is going to be cantaloupe, coconut, and banana oatmeal, actually quinoa. Then, we will fry some fish; there you go, hearty and fresh."

"You can't live on all this good stuff, right? It's like we found a garden of ice cream," Harold asked.

"No, that's totally wrong," Alex said,

"you could live on all of this."

Joy nodded and said, "You just got more vitamins and healthy stuff at this meal than we've had for weeks."

"Who did this?" Scott indicated the garden with his arms.

"You're the curious one, Scott. Figure it out by tomorrow so we know."

Scott could only grin at Alex and belch. He laughed, and it was one of the few real laughs he had experienced since the nightmares began on the island. "Food has made me feel crazy-happy. I guess the healthy stuff does work."

They stayed by the fire and close to the crack between the boulders and were unbothered, giving them some deep, undisturbed sleep. Each felt the effects of a vitamin-fuelled meal and a restful sleep, things they had craved.

In the morning after another good meal, Scott climbed the highest boulder and followed the rocks a while, looking over the land and sea.

After a while, he climbed down and explored a section of beach that interested him, yet, he was still unbothered by creatures. What he found both explained some things, added more mysteries, and at one point terrified him, but he appreciated all of it as reality.

At one point, he felt it was foolish to go onto a section of the beach alone, but he did, venturing far from the boulders and finding himself unhappy with his discovery, but also satisfied that he had necessary information.

"We thought something got you," Alex frowned as Scott returned. "You can't go off alone like that."

"Sorry, nothing got me, but something got the people who planted your garden."

"All of them? Do you think?" Joy asked.

"I think so or maybe some died later, but I know who it was, though I can't explain it. Stu would love this: what I found."

Alex was in lower spirits than the night before even though the dinner was delicious and varied again. Something troubled him, and Scott could see it was something they all knew and were mulling over. It was part of the reason Alex was so upset, and what caused Scott to venture out alone.

Scott looked at the rest and said, "What's up?"

Mattie breathed deeply, "It's crazy because we know those poor sailors washed up from their ship that went down right off the beach where we live. *Cyclops.* While we gathered food, we explored, too. We found things…"

"Things?"

Alex took over and told him, "We found personal things and items from the *Cyclops*, Scott. I know we saw the remains of the shipwreck, and we saw the ocean toss bodies out a few week ago, but somehow, those sailors from *Cyclops* were also here, just like Littleton's boat being in two places five years apart."

Mattie said, "What we found is older, though. On our beach was a newer wreck as if the ship went down right then and not a long time ago."

Scott didn't argue or look shocked. Silently nodding as he listened, he asked, "Would you say this garden was planted almost a hundred years ago? Is it that old?"

"I think so. The fennel and ginger...the original plants look that old. They were cut back a lot, but haven't been cut again for..." Alex said, looking confused.

"Twenty years?" asked Scott.

"Yeah. Okay, what did you find?" Joy asked Scott.

"Three things. Some of these boulders were moved by manpower: ropes and logs and many, many, men working. Most were here already, but to get set up like this in a sort of boulder-fence means they had help. I mean someone moved these boulders, and it wasn't giants," said Scott.

"Okay, no giants," Alex agreed.

"Second, way, way over there, mostly on the beach but in the water some is a gigantic ship. It's rusted badly and in rough shape. It's about a hundred years old, and I was able to read the name only slightly through the rust."

"*Cyclops*," said Alex.

"It sure is. Back in the first part of the twentieth century, just as you and Stu said, the ship vanished from out there and crashed here," Scott explained. "It crashed where we live on the beach, *and* it crashed here on this beach. Where we live, the ship went down off the shore, and only bodies and debris washed up. Here, the entire ship crashed onto the shoreline."

"This makes no sense," Joy whispered.

Scott agreed but said he felt they were getting closer to answers. "Neither did Littleton's boat. I think we might have more mysteries before we understand the one we have now. There's something huge going on here, and I'm not sure our minds are capable of understanding anything."

"Like infinity. Humans try, but we can't really get the magnitude of infinity," Alex said.

"They lived here, didn't they, Scott?" Joy asked.

"Yes, and I think they lived here a long time. On the other side of the wreck, there is a horrible, pitiful pile of human bones and I think there was a fight with some dinosaurs there on the beach. There are dino bones, but I can't tell them apart except these are big and they had pointed teeth."

"All those men," Alex said softly.

"They were here and they died. This garden didn't save them from predators, and then, a hundred years later, in a storm, *Cyclops* and men aboard it crashed again, but on our end of the island. The time we saw, the ship broke apart and sank, and no one survived."

Alex closed one eye and warded off a headache. He wanted a drink of the whiskey they brought but held himself back. Once they are dead, the ship, boar, or plane can come back again, maybe in a year, or five, or ten. They've gone at least twice, right?"

Scott nodded.

"Jada once told me something strange. She said she had *de je vu*, and felt as if she had been there before and had nightmares about dinosaurs," Alex said.

"Benny has had them, but Amy said she doesn't, and Littleton said he never did, but he said he had a nightmare about drowning," Scott told them. "You're thinking that they have a hidden memory of their deaths?"

Alex shrugged.

"I found two things I sure didn't like: a footprint in the mud and a lone feather." Scott brought out a brown feather that was tipped with an iridescent bright blue. "Big Brown is in the area, or has been recently."

"Following us?" asked Mattie.

"I don't know. It can't be very old, though." Scott told Mattie.

"I hate that *shitty-saur*," Joy said, making everyone smile.

"At least we know now and won't be surprised," Alex said.

They spent a total of three nights in the garden, picking and packing up the fresh food.

They became determined that they might even push for everyone to move there because it was safer. Several acres in size, it had fresh water and gardens, and was protected from predators by the boulders. It would be far better as a camp if they moved what they could and managed to get everything inside.

They needed an engineer; Littleton was in a related field and could be helpful, Alex thought and then told everyone else. He liked the idea of moving their camp. "Just like Eden, we can have all this food, and while there will be a reptile or two here, at least it won't be a big one trying to eat us."

Back on the beach, they saw the places Scott had already found and moved along, always wondering what they would find at the next turn.

The next surprise could be wonderful, or a nightmare, as it was most often.

Chapter 16: Exploration

They walked during the day and slept at night, always on guard and lonesome for the safe, garden of food.

One afternoon, they found a small herd of long-necked dinosaurs wading and swimming in the ocean's waves. The babies surfed in the water and then rolled on the sand when they landed on the shoreline. Alex said he had never seen anything like them but suspected they were a very small version of a brachiosaur.

"Benny was right in saying the island couldn't support many of the real giants. It's a very small version, but unlike any we know."

"Kind of like the island makes up different kinds of dinosaurs?" Joy asked.

"No, not at all. Fossils are very amazing, but a creature doesn't die and drop and then make a fossil, see. The conditions have got to be right. I imagine there are hundreds of different types of dinosaurs that archeologists have never found evidence of," Alex said. "It doesn't surprise me at all to find some we never even imagined."

"Shhh. Don't scare them away," Mattie warned. "Be quiet."

The adults were no longer than twelve feet from nose to tail. Mattie enjoyed watching them and thought they were like funny cows. She asked if they could corral them and raise them like cattle.

Her question left Scott speechless.

"They'd draw predators," Alex said. "Besides, who would kill such funny looking, sweet-faced, goofy creatures? They don't give milk. Nah. Let's leave them alone, okay?"

His answer to *what* would kill them was in the jungle, watching the mini-brachs. A pack of strange bird-like dinosaurs chittered, peeked, and ducked at the edge of the jungle. Their eyes were large and were about thigh-high to the men, but looked more like birds than anything except for their sharp teeth and sharp claws on the forelimbs and hind legs.

Greenish yellow feathers covered them, almost making them seem to have fat wings, but their forelegs were far more dexterous than mere wings would be. Plumage of yellow and green topped the crests on their heads, making them almost comical in appearance.

"They keep watching. They want to attack but aren't sure what *we* are. What are they?" Tom asked.

"*Bird-a-saurs*?" asked Harold.

Alex shook his head at Harold and said, "Velociraptors."

"Oh, shit. I thought those things were much bigger, but they're lethal, right?" Harold was afraid and watched the creatures more carefully. "Aren't those the worst dinos of all?"

"It would be like tangling with a bobcat if one of them gets you, but no, the movies were way off. They seem about normal size, but actually, these are big for true velociraptors. See the feathers? The movies didn't get that right, either."

"Are they dangerous, Alex? So far, you've given a movie review," Scott said dryly. He was amused.

"Well, they're somewhat fast, but are nothing compared to troodons or Utahraptors. I think they're fairly stupid, too, but they could take down a mini-brach if they wanted to and probably will."

A pair of the velociraptors stalked down the sand quietly, snorting softly to see what their prey would do and what reactions they'd get. Alex lunged forward with his spear and poked one of the creatures in its wing, drawing blood and causing the animal to squeal angrily as it backpedaled.

The others snapped their heads forward and hissed.

"Don't back down. Stay aggressive," Alex suggested. He thought they could be scared away.

"*I'm* scared," Joy screamed. "They're all over the place. Damnit, Alex, do something."

"Don't show your fear. If they sense or smell fear, they may attack, and there are enough in the pack to hurt or kill one of us easily. They'll try to separate us, and once we are isolated, we will be food.

Stay together, and keep moving. If they get close, stab them," added Scott as he stabbed with his spear, hitting none of the animals, but forcing them to back away again.

Tom was able to stab another one in its chest, causing the rest of the pack to snap and bite at the wounded beast. Once the velociraptors were distracted, the humans scurried by and moved down the beach. Shortly, they were out of sight of the little monsters and when the velociraptors didn't follow, the humans relaxed.

Whatever happened to the small brachiosaurs and the velociraptors, no one knew, but the group wasn't concerned; at least they were safe and free to keep moving. Mattie was disappointed that there was no sign of her son, but also glad they didn't find his body.

"Cindy didn't mention the garden of boulders or anything this way. That tells me they were more inland," Scott said.

"Then, why are we here? We should be looking inland," Harold argued.

"I never said we were going to track those kids. I said I was coming this way. You said you would look for Jody," Scott scowled. "I said if we found them, we'd deal with them in some way. I never planned to do anything but look around."

Mattie and Harold traded glances but didn't argue.

The next day, they found what Scott had been curious about weeks before. There was a deep swath from the beach to the jungle where trees were broken away or knocked down as if a giant had pushed them away. They saw what had shocked and scared them almost two weeks before during one of the big storms.

A big black crater ruined the green lushness. Broken trees lined it, and most were singed black. In the center covering a half mile in each direction were burned metal beams, shapeless, charred lumps, ashes from burned trees, disturbed soil, and the few remains of a once-grand, once-enormous jetliner.

This was where the airplane crashed and burned for days after the violent storm. While the debris was far too blackened and broken up to identify the remains of the plane, there was enough left to be sure that the airplane was modern.

Scott thought it was possible that the plane was from a time the survivors had not yet reached. It might be several years in the future, a crash that had not happened in their time.

"That kind of thinking hurts my head," Joy complained. "I liked it better when the past was really the past."

"Me, too," Tom said, "and the plane was probably loaded with passengers."

Harold said something that was unnecessary but appropriate, "I know that no one survived that, but at least they didn't suffer long."

Chapter 17: Misery

The sand was a smaller strip in this area and was littered with rocks and old timbers, twisted metal, and junk that had been washed ashore. It was an ugly beach because of all the trash, some of it very old but some fresh. A few bleached bones were buried by the sand and licked by the tides as water rose and fell.

For a full two weeks, they hid in a cave they found in the cliffs above the beach. The cliffs were filled with caves, some small and some very large, but they camped in one that was roomy and easily defended.

After the first night spent in the cave, they were forced to put off leaving as a storm blew in, beginning normally enough with thunder, lightning, and rain, but becoming worse and more ominous over the next twenty-four hours. The yellow mist covered the ocean and tinted the clouds, while the wind wailed and whistled through the cave system, sounding ghostly. Everyone wondered what the storm might bring to the beach and feared seeing wreckage.

The group was glad for their supplies and unwilling to venture out into the bad weather. They hoped the storm would pass, but it lingered. Sometimes it seemed normal for a long time, but it always turned strange again. The sky always looked yellowish when the storm increased in intensity.

Joy moaned that she thought the storm might last forever, but Tom kept saying that he felt the island had frequent storms and that this was most likely the rainy season, so they would just have to wait it out. Having often sailed on the yacht with his father, Tom was accustomed to times in the tropics when storm seasons raged for weeks at a time, but they always tried to avoid those times.

Mattie stayed wrapped in a blanket that never lost the damp feeling even though she sat next to the fire. The air was always chilly and wet.

"At least we have food, right?" Alex said.

"And it won't rain forever," Scott said, hoping that was true.

At times, he stood at the mouth of the cave and listened to the wind and thought he heard louder crashes from far away. He said he felt the storm wouldn't cause the biggest predators to slow down because they were hungry and needed to hunt for food. The activities of the carnivores kept the prey from getting too complacent.

More than once they saw blazing fires that dimmed quickly with the rain, but Alex said that they were the fires from plane crashes in the jungle or on a nearby beach.

"It's active right now, isn't it?" Alex asked.

"The weather?" asked Tom.

"The island," Alex told him, "it's been loading up for over a month now. The storms have been worse and closer together."

"Storm season," Tom added.

"Yeah, but *here*, that means something else, doesn't it?" asked Alex as he began to ration their food, hoping that they wouldn't be stuck in the cave forever even if it were safe from most of the dinosaurs.

A few unfortunate compys tried to take shelter in the cave, and Scott and Alex pegged them with rocks, adding their meat to the rations.

"Even the animals hate these storms," Mattie said. She ate her portion of the compsognathus meat and thought of broiled chicken; it tasted good, but she was tired of the cave and endless boredom. All there was to do was sleep.

After the first week, a sense of depression swept over them since they had to remain inside the cave. Scott worried about their mental state as much as he hated the chill and dampness.

Living in a cave was not pleasant, and he wondered why Mattie's husband and son had chosen it over staying with their airplane. It felt like Scott and his friends were already becoming less advanced the longer they remained.

"You aren't a caveman," Alex said.

"How'd you know what I was thinking?" Scott asked, surprised. He was sharpening a spear tip and imagined doing that every night by the light of the fire.

"I can see your face and the way you keep looking at the rocks. I feel the same way. Because we were excited about food and are now depressed over the storms, we are reactionary."

"I feel like I'm devolving," said Scott.

"Maybe we all are," Alex said.

"Does the wind sound weaker?" Joy asked. It was the same question they had asked dozens of times.

"Maybe." Scott thought that this time the storm was less violent, but he had been fooled days before. "You hate being out there on the run. You hate being cooped up. It's one of the other. Relax."

"I hate being stuck here," Joy said. She felt like complaining about everything; it was something to do, at least. She knew it aggravated Tom, but she couldn't stop herself. She wasn't smart like Alex or strong like Tom and Scott. Harold and Mattie were quiet and depressing, so Joy entertained herself by whining.

She didn't explain that she hated the storms and that the rain was holding them hostage. She hated the cave's dampness, the bugs that crawled around the cave, the dirtiness that was always there, the booming thunder, and the fact that there might be more ships and planes wrecking.

The next day was calmer, the yellow faded from the sea and sky, and the day after that was clear. It would be a while before everything dried out. The storms might return, but the group could not stand to stay inside the cave another day, they had to find fresh food, and they had to be active again. They craved the sounds of the ocean and the chance to wash themselves.

Joy let the sun warm her face and reveled in the warmth. "It feels so good out here in the light."

They fished and gathered fruit but returned to the cliffs to spend the night in a new cave, and as they traveled this section of the island, they wondered how long the cliffs and caves would last before there was no longer shelter. They hated being trapped in the caves by the storms, but liked sleeping in them at night so they were safe. They had both mind-sets.

"We've been lucky. We keep finding places to stay when we need them. Maybe our luck will hold," Scott said. "I wouldn't mind having caves as shelter, but it feels wrong to stay in them for very long."

"We're never satisfied, are we?" Tom mused. "I think it's because we just want to be back home."

"Home is gone. We're not going back. Home's gone," replied Scott.

"Scott, you sound like Stu," Joy protested. "I know he's your brother, Tom, but he's an ass most times."

"I can't argue that. Scott is right, though. *Home* is gone," Tom said. He put his arm around Joy and let her sniffle for a while.

Mattie and Harold looked uncomfortable.

"We've been lucky that there are fewer predators here. There's nothing for them along the cliffs, but that doesn't mean they don't look for food," said Alex as he watched the trees.

Mattie jumped as a flock of birds burst from the trees and a roar echoed. She was tired of combing through trash on the beach, as she stepped over an old ship's rotten mast.

She hated retreating to the caves at night, but the thought of being out in the open was terrifying after becoming used to the safety the cliffs offered. She stopped to kick the piece of rotten wood, hating the truths of a bent reality that it represented.

"There's something in the trees," Alex said.

"There always is," Joy shrugged as she told him that. Her head snapped around as another roar sounded, and this closer one scared her. She moved closer to Tom. "Not again."

"*Always* again. They never stop trying to get a free meal," Mattie said.

"We aren't free," Joy said nervously.

"What are they?" Harold asked.

"How could Alex know?" Scott responded.

"I know this; it's big," Alex snapped. They kept asking him what was stomping and roaring behind them but hidden by trees and rocks. He couldn't see what kind of dinosaur was stalking them, only that there were several of them and that they were large predators, which moved along the same trail as the humans.

"Cliffs or the wreck?" Scott asked. He didn't know if they could make it to a cave before the big creatures got to the beach, but wreckage from some plane was closer, and they could fight from there if attacked.

"The plane…" Mattie ran towards it.

A large section of the middle of a jetliner was dented and crumpled in spots, but mostly intact. One end of the middle was sealed like a tin can, and the other end was flush against the face of the cliff.

 Unfortunately, other parts of the plane were torn away. One wing was sheared away and stood tip-up in the ocean, a few dozen yards off the beach. The nose section was separated and smashed into the base of the cliffs, and the tail section was missing.

Scott was concerned about the animals that were stalking them, but he felt something new. Curiosity returned to him, and there was a familiarity he couldn't place.

Along with all the mysterious planes and ships that they had found crashed on the island, this was just another one of the many mysteries and losses, but this wreckage seemed different.

Harold ran and then stopped in his tracks, scaring the rest. He slid to his knees and leaned over to vomit. Mattie stopped running and stood next to Harold as she stared at the airplane, her head tilted as she tried to breathe through her own nausea and shock. Her skin looked waxy.

"That plane…" said Harold.

"Yeah, it's ours," Mattie said as she gave Harold help so he could stand, and then they walked closer, ready to find a way to use the wreckage as a hiding spot or as a fortress.

Scott rubbed his jaw and sorted out the image he stared at. A ladder made of ropes and branches and held in place by the sand that nested around the plane led to the opened door.

Because the wreck carved out a depression in the beach when the plane plowed in as some sort of landing, the doorway wasn't as high above the surface of the beach as it would have been on tarmac.

"Go. Climb," Alex ordered.

Behind them, a pair of ceratosaurs lumbered onto the beach, roaring and stomping. They were nervous about the airplane, which kept them from rushing at the human prey, but the pair refused to hang back for long because they were hungry. The pair of dinosaurs made a decision and ran. They moved faster than the humans could, but the hungry carnivores were too late.

Once everyone was up the ladder and in the airplane, Alex yanked the door closed.

One of the ceratosaurs raked its nasal horn across the underbelly of the airplane, making a high-pitched whine as bone and metal met.

Another one bumped the plane several times, trying to frighten the prey into running, but inside, the humans slid to the floor and waited. There was no way to get to the humans unless the creatures tore apart the metal of the airplane.

"Can they get in?" Joy asked.

"I hope not. I doubt it," Alex said.

Joy jumped up and slammed one of the plastic coverings over the window as she saw a dinosaur's eye looking inside. She hated being watched, so she curled up against Tom once she was sure the creatures couldn't see her anymore.

"Ceratosaurs. They'll get bored and wander away, I think. They probably have a nest in the jungle close to a pond hidden by the trees. They can hunt better closer to their homes. They'll leave."

"Why are they here bothering us?" Tom asked.

"Because of the storm," Alex said, "their scent trails are all screwed up, so they're looking for anything they can hunt and eat."

The animals sniffed around curiously and looked for opportunities to feed. A strong scent of death was there, but it was diminished because of the recent rains, and the dinosaurs lost interest rapidly. After the pair of ceratosaurs finished bumping the plane and exploring, the roars stopped.

Mattie stayed in place a while, sitting by Scott, but then she got up and began to look around as if searching the interior of the plane for something. She ran her fingers over the stamped seat numbers and took hesitant steps. Several times she paused and looked confused, but then moved again.

Harold followed behind her.

Scott understood that the airplane seemed familiar. He watched Mattie and Harold, and then he looked at Alex who nodded to him.

"What am I missing?" Tom asked.

"We've been here before. Not *here* exactly, but kind of here. It's like the *Violet Marie*. It was beached, and we saw it, touched it, and stood right there with the wreckage, and then Littleton and his people showed up along with a different…"

"Scenario," Alex supplied the word.

"Right. We don't know what the first scenario entailed, but in the one we saw, Littleton, Jade, Amy, and Benny survived, and we found them. I suspect that may mean that they didn't make it the…well…other time."

"Because even if this is a crazy island, we can't be two places at once because then we would have a real paradox. It doesn't work even in the weirdest, shittiest scenarios," Alex said.

"I still don't get it," said Tom, as he looked from Scott and Alex to Harold and Mattie, "and what are they doing?"

"Tom, we saw two versions of what might have happened to the *Violet Marie*. I guess there may be a hundred variations or a thousand. In some cases, I bet the boat didn't wash up at all. I think that maybe the boat has been in the storm a thousand times over ten thousand or millions of years. Millions. That explains the dinosaurs' timeline."

Tom nodded but didn't understand. He wondered what Scott thought about all of this, but never had he been fond of science fiction, and now it seemed to Tom that he was right in the middle of a sci-fi movie or book. He didn't like this because it felt unrealistic to him. It was easier to nod and wonder than seriously try to make sense of everything. He didn't understand Scott and Alex's need to explain.

Alex drew an imaginary line on the floor. He said that was how most people considered time. He pointed and said that was where they were in time now. Then, he drew an imaginary square above the line and used his finger to touch several spots within the square. "This is more of what we have been thinking. Each spot is *us* in time, but at different times. Follow?"

"That makes sense. Okay," said Tom as he frowned. It did make sense in a strange way.

Alex drew the square again a few inches above the one he pretended to draw on the floor.

He repeated that several more times, going higher and sometimes drawing more to one side or the other. He mimed his actions and made them dramatic, as he said, "Those spots are us in time, but in other scenarios. Do you see? It's a cube with layers. They all overlap, and the overlapped point is the island. The storm."

"I think I'm following what you're saying. Like the *Cyclops*. Scenarios. In some versions, they crashed here or *there*. It's a cube. Dimensions, right?" Tom asked. He was curious as the explanation began to make sense to him. He viewed this as almost a mathematical issue and smiled.

"We have a winner!" Scott said. He was glad Alex showed them because he understood a little more, not that he understood everything about the situation. "Alex, you get this more than we do. What is out here?" He indicated a spot far from the cube by pointing far away in the air.

"Home?" Tom asked.

"I don't know," said Alex, chuckling, "but wow, Scott, way to blow my physics lessons.

Seriously, I don't know. I don't know if we can meet ourselves. I just know there *are* rules, but we don't know these rules because they are *done to* us. We don't have to know them or understand them, but we have to follow them. We're locked into them, I mean."

"Locked?" Tom asked.

Alex thought and then said, "I mean there is gravity. Some people understand the physics of gravity, but even if we don't, we don't float up in the air, right? We are locked into the rules even if we never study them."

Scott looked over to where Mattie and Harold walked, both leaning over and looking at seat numbers and muttering to one another as they talked. They stopped again.

"Harold, oh, I was sitting right here. Jody was beside me. Here. I feel like I'm seeing a ghost."

"No ghosts, but Mattie, did you bleed that much? Look at these stains. Was it Jody? These seats are covered."

Mattie was confused. She looked back at the others and shook her head. "I don't understand. I wasn't hurt except for a few bruises and cuts. I didn't bleed this much, and neither did Jody."

"There are no bodies," said Alex as he stood looking around again. "This crash is bad, but someone lived, and he removed the bodies. Maybe even buried them?"

"But the blood…" Mattie said, breaking off to rub her head.

"In this scenario, you or Jody were very badly hurt, Mattie. It's possible that you died. That's what we've been talking about. Various outcomes."

"I died, Scott? Is that it? My, God, I feel dizzy."

Harold reached out an arm to help hold Mattie on her feet.

"That's kind of normal when we try to resolve thinking about infinity and things that are beyond our comprehension," said Alex as he suggested they leave the airplane because it was now safe to go outside and because Mattie was pale and sick.

"What about you, Harold? Should we look for your seat, or do you prefer not to know?" Tom asked.

Harold sniffed and rubbed his eyes. He was overwhelmed but pointed and said, "See how the tail is ripped off? What do you think became of those folks?"

"Oh, no question. Those poor bastards all died. Torn apart. Why?" Tom asked.

Alex made a squeaking sound, and his eyes were huge.

"What?" Tom was flummoxed.

Harold stared at the sand as they walked. In a second, he spoke softly, "I was one of those poor bastards, Tom. I was in the tail section."

Chapter 18: Predators

"Now what, Scott?" Alex asked.

They walked for days, nervously camping in groves of trees after they left the caves and beach behind. The island curved around to the left, and they followed that for a few days and then angled into the trees when they saw that the beach never changed. There was sand, water, and occasionally the remains of old ship wrecks and big bones.

After a half day of walking in the jungle by using animal paths, they grew tired of the constant threat of attacks and the wet trees that caught moisture and rained it down on them, even when the days were cloudless. It was far too hot and damp within the interior of the island.

"I whined about the cold cave. I wish it wasn't so hot," Joy said, wiping sweat from her face and trying to catch her breath.

"We can go back toward the beach, use the caves there, and backtrack, I suppose," Scott suggested.

"I thought you wanted to see the whole island or find answers," Tom said.

"I saw part of it. It's pretty much the same thing every day, isn't it? And it's huge. I paid attention, and I think we barely saw any of it. Watching the sun, I kept track, and we were still going north. Face the facts; this place is far bigger than we thought. Who knows what happens on the other parts," Alex told them.

"It's just too much to think we can handle anything except our small part," Scott agreed.

"If we can handle even that. I don't know if we have any control," Alex said.

"I could be dead in a dozen places," Mattie added. She had been depressed for days.

"I wish we didn't know anything," Harold said.

Scott shrugged and said, "You knew I was looking for answers."

"Did you get the ones you wanted?"

Scott looked at Alex and said, "Sure, we found a place to live, to be safer, and to be where there is food. We know others lived here for decades and survived. We understand much more. I can't say I like it all, but at least we *know*."

"I don't wanna know anything else," Joy said.

They found the remains of a fire just off an animal trail and then another. Both were several weeks old, cold, overgrown, and almost washed away. Scott wished this were something they hadn't found and didn't know about because it reminded him that there was a predator out in the jungle that was human.

Scott and Alex walked ahead and examined the second campsite, motioning the others to stay back. The debris left at the old fire made both men worry. Alex identified several human bones: legs, rib cages, and arms. Scott and he gave the bones a cursory burial under some soil, branches, and old leaves.

"What do you think?" asked Scott.

Alex didn't know what to tell Scott. He felt it was obvious that someone had cooked and eaten another human at the campsite. They didn't know who did it, but had a reasonable idea. "I think they're some sick sons of bitches."

Scott and Alex told the others what they found and tried to keep Mattie from sinking lower into her depression, but Mattie felt it had to be her son's group. She wanted to find Jody, but also wished never to see him again. "I wish it was different."

Two days later, there was no way to avoid confronting reality. Scott almost shoved a spear into the boy who ran into their camp, but stopped him to ask questions instead, "Who the hell are you? Are you alone?"

"Just us. We don't mean no harm," the boy said. "I'm Danny, and this is Marita, Mari. Please don't kill us."

Scott wasn't sure what to do. Alex looked torn between protecting themselves and showing mercy. He was also curious about the boy and girl. "Answer everything truthfully if you want to be spared."

"Okay. Anything, but don't kill us."

Mattie jumped to her feet and approached the pair, and reaching out as if afraid they weren't real. "Mari? Little Mari, and Danny, you look the same. So handsome."

Danny blinked. Tears filled his eyes as he fought to keep from crying with fear. "What is this shit? What kind of trick? We just wanted to find other people…"

Scott had to work to keep them calm and get the group to ask only one question at a time and then wait for answers. Everyone wanted to talk at once, and the group was emotionally charged. "Settle down."

"But, Mattie?" Danny asked, his eyes hurt and shining with tears.

Scott managed to find out that Danny and Mari were from Harold and Mattie's plane and were a part of the group of children who left the plane. They remembered Mattie and were shocked to see her standing before them as if she had betrayed them.

Danny and Mari had been with Jody's group, but recently had left to go off alone, saying they couldn't live with the way Jody ran the group. The couple had survived, as had Jody, after being attacked by Big Brown and the troodons, and were surprised to learn that Cindy had gone to the survivor's beach camp and died there.

"Cindy was really afraid of Jody," Danny admitted. "We never got a good look at your camp, and we sure didn't know Mattie was there. I can imagine Cindy trying to get away."

Mari never spoke, just crossed herself repeatedly and muttered. She was pale beneath her suntan and used her long, dark hair to cover her face, as she watched the group with real fear in her eyes. She looked at Harold and Mattie with terror.

"I won't hurt you," Mattie told Mari.

"You are a ghost."

Mattie remembered how she felt in the second version of her airplane and understood about ghosts and how it felt to be haunted. Mari was afraid of her and Harold. That was fine. Mattie was scared of herself and of what the island did and how it changed life, death, and reality.

Scott knew his group considered revenge on the pair for being cannibals, but Mattie and Harold were somewhat sympathetic. Alex was as curious as Scott, who tried to calm Danny and Mari while he told them that they were safe, but Danny shivered with fear the whole time they talked.

Back at home camp, there would be several who hated and feared Danny and Mari. It might be best to refuse to let them stay with Scott's group.

"Danny, I feel like we're missing something here. Parts of this make no sense," Scott said. "Tell me your story."

"I can't explain it. It makes no sense. See, back a long time ago, we were at the cave with Jim, and we drank the water in the pool, but it wasn't good water."

"No, it was full of natural steroids," Alex said.

Danny waved that off, saying, "That ain't it. You'll think I'm crazy, but something bad happened back then. Mattie, please don't get too upset, but these dinosaurs come after us, and it was different back then."

Danny explained as best he could, stopping often to wipe sweat and tears and shaking as he talked.

Jody and Ricky led the children as they left the main camp located in a cave. All of the children were aggressive, and Danny confirmed that the girls went through puberty rapidly, but he said that while they were wild and lawless, they never harmed a human.

Scott encouraged him to continue. This wasn't how Mattie had told the story. "We know your group...Jody and the rest...they killed people. They killed Lori."

"Let me go from the start," Danny pled.

"Please," Scott said.

One day, Danny said they decided that the group of children would meet with Jim, the leader of the adult group from the cave where they made their home and the other adults to try to find a common ground.

The children wanted discipline again. Like children knowing they had been mischievous, these children prepared to be blamed and yelled at by their parents. They needed the adults.

Meeting on neutral ground, the children and adults began to talk, and both sides immediately felt hopeful, but everything went to hell almost immediately when a pack of Utahraptors attacked, slaughtering almost everyone. In lowering their weapons for a peaceful meeting, the group had forgotten to be careful of an attack from dinosaurs.

"I'm so sorry, Mattie, but Jody and Ricky were killed. Those asshole dinos took both back to their nest or territory, whatever it's called. Took the remains, I mean."

"They died? But…"

"The attack was huge. It was so sudden and big that no one could do anything. Most everyone was slaughtered," said Danny as he wept. "My father was torn to pieces."

Mattie's jaw dropped as she found the words to ask, "How can that be? Cindy said Jody and Ricky were alive, and Stu said Jodie and Ricky attacked Lori and killed her? We heard they were cannibals."

"We found the bones, Danny. We know what went on," Scott told him. "Wasn't that Jody?"

"It was, and it wasn't."

"Huh?" Scott asked.

"I *know* all that," said Danny again, as he thought the group would think he was crazy, but he continued. Most of those that the Utahraptors attacked were killed. Dozens. A few adults were injured badly, but Danny didn't know what happened to them. Of the children, a few were left alive but wounded, and Danny and Mari were the only two to escape.

"Jody?"

"He died, Mattie. I'm sorry. Later, those that ran with us…most of them with us died, and we…we had to leave them because we had to run away. We didn't think we'd be welcomed at the plane with the Air Marshal."

Instead of going to the airplane, Danny and Mari made their way west.

Eventually, only the pair was left alive because various packs of predators attacked and killed the remaining members of the group. "It was just us, and we were lonely. It hurt every day."

One day, they met a new group made up of young adults and teenagers who was camping around a small fire. They were relieved to find more humans.

"It's crazy, and we kind of went nuts because they're at the fire, were Jody and Ricky! Just like they had never died. Mari, well, she ain't talked much since then 'cause it hit us so hard.

She and I were struck dumb by it, and I guess I was hysterical a while. They were calm and let us rest. We didn't know what to believe, and Jody had to do something. He took us to see this plane crash on the beach not far from here."

"We saw it. It's your plane," Scott said. "Although that's confusing, right?"

"Yeah, how can it be there and *also* be in the trees where I was? I remember only that I was in the trees in that crash, but I saw the wreck on the beach, too. Jody and Ricky told us that they were in *that* crash; the crash on the beach was all they remembered and not the other one," said Danny.

Alex nodded and added, "It's insane. The people that were from the beach crash didn't remember or know of the other crash where they died. Danny and Mari don't know about the beach crash because in the beach one, they died. We only would have the memories of the one where we were alive. I mean that we wouldn't have memories of any other scenario."

"Why?" asked Scott.

Alex stared hard at Scott and said, "Because those are the rules here. We start over each time, and each experience is new. I don't make the rules, but am just telling you what I think they are."

"We forget?" Scott asked.

"We never *are* there. Not when it resets."

Danny went on without being asked, "Jody said that they watched the other people with them bury a bunch of us...me and Mari. Jody told us a terrible story about his mother...about you, Mattie."

Jody told Danny and Mari that his mother was injured badly in the crash and died. She had lost her arm and bled to death. "Jody saw her...*you* died. He couldn't handle it. He was furious."

"My poor baby..."

After that, Jody began leading the group, and many were killed in dinosaur attacks and by other things until a group of just young people was left. We didn't know how to tell him that you were alive in another..." continued Danny.

"Scenario?" Alex offered.

"We didn't know the words to use anyway.

Jody was calm for a while, but he had already chosen the ways of the group. He didn't act crazy, but he was always angry and always hungry. We did bad things because Jody said we should; he wasn't right in the head. We went to spy a little on your camp and came back this way. We wandered and killed because Jody said we had to. We done been attacked so many times..."

"By a big brown dinosaur and troodons?" asked Alex.

"Yeah. Cindy and a bunch run off. We ran, too. Then Mari and I ran away again from Jody's group because they...well...if one of us dies, they eat the person. He thinks that makes them not able to return, yanno? It's the way he thinks. He don't want people coming back," Danny said as he violently shivered again.

"That makes no sense. Eating people wouldn't change the rules of physics here," said Alex, insulted by Jody's beliefs.

"How is that possible? Maybe Jody wasn't killed," Mattie said.

"He was, though. I saw it myself. Before, in the other way, he was a good person, Mattie, and he'd never have got us to do what we did. He wasn't that way. He talked about you back then and said he was gonna visit you at the airplane.

The *other* Jody, see this is crazy talk, but it's the truth. I swear it is, but *he* wasn't the same," said Danny, not knowing how to explain this very well.

"He was different in the new version?" Alex asked. "Jody was okay in the first scenario, but the water messed him up, yet, he was still okay. Then, he died, and I'm sorry, Mattie, but he did. Your version of him died."

Scott nodded and said, "Keep going."

"The storm brought a new plane wreck scenario. In the other one, Mattie and Harold died, and Jody became irrational. He became a monster because everything was altered. There were no caves, no steroid water, no mother, and none of the other stuff. It was *different*."

"What does that mean?" Mattie asked. "My son…"

"It means that the Jody you knew never ate people or killed them. He *wasn't* bad. In the other version, you died horribly, and it unhinged his mind. He became a bad person."

Mattie stared at Alex. "But he is still my child. My son."

"Yes, but he's not the same," said Alex and then asked Danny, "did you know they killed Lori?"

"Yeah, it's how they are. They got wilder and weirder every day. That's why Cindy used the attack to run away. It's why Mari and I ran away. If they had caught us, we're dead."

Tom coughed to break the mood and said, "This has blown my mind. I thought I understood this like Alex explained, but…"

"But it's insane," Joy added, "and it makes no sense."

"Imagine how we felt," Danny said.

"Do you feel better or worse, Mattie?" Scott asked gently.

"I don't know how I feel. Confused. Sad. What will we do now?"

"I think we have to find them and deal with this. I know this is upsetting to you, and we don't understand it either, but we have to face Jody. The new version."

Mattie nodded to Scott. She swallowed hard and had a desperate look in her eyes. She might nod and seem to agree, but in her head, she was trying to figure out how this could be fixed so she had her son back. As a mother, she couldn't let him go.

Four days later, they found Jody's group in an unfortunate situation.

Chapter 19: Battle

Because they could hear the beginning of a battle somewhere ahead of them, Alex suggested that they skirt far around the sounds of dinosaurs roaring and stomping. Although they had backtracked toward the beach and stayed away from the deeper parts of the jungle, the animal path they were following ran directly into an area, a heavily populated section of the land.

As quietly as possible, the group crept through the trees, trying to get to the beach where it might be safer. Mattie stopped and yanked her head back in the other direction as she listened. Beside her, Danny and Mari did the same.

"That's Jody!" Mattie whispered.

"No, it isn't," Tom said, "so we need to keep going."

"I heard his voice. Didn't you hear him, Danny?"

Danny dropped his eyes. He didn't want to go into a clearing where dinosaurs were already making horrible noises and preparing to fight. He was scared of the beasts. In addition, he sure didn't want to go where Jody and Ricky were because they were sure to be angry that Danny and Mari ran away. Danny figured that one way or another, either the feral children or the dinosaurs would kill and eat him.

"Danny?" asked Mattie.

"I guess it was a dino squealing. It wasn't him, Mattie."

From beyond the trees, a young man yelled, his words garbled, but Mattie knew it was Jody. "You little liar," she told Danny.

"He can't win, no matter what, Mattie. Look..." Scott wasn't sure exactly what he planned to say.

He didn't have to decide. Mattie suddenly slapped at Scott and dashed away down another trail, running as fast as she could. Scott felt her shirt slip through his hands as he made a grab for her, and might have stopped her had she not slapped his hands.

For a second, Scott didn't move. Logic told him to take his group and leave the area because it was far too dangerous to try to save anyone from the warring animals.

It was also a fact that he was less inclined to intercede, because to him, Jody was a feral beast in his own right, a cannibal, and a lost cause. Jody needed to be dealt with; in fact, Stu planned to hunt the children down and kill them anyway.

Harold made a choice. Bravely, he ran after Mattie, yelling that he was going to help make sure she wasn't injured.

Scott thought that Harold was either very foolish or very brave and loyal. "Damnit. Okay. I'm going. Stay here if you want to be safe." He couldn't make the choice for the entire group. Following Mattie and Harold was a bad plan.

Alex and Tom immediately joined Scott, and they ran with him as he followed Mattie. Behind them, Joy, Danny, and Mari followed.

The clearing was total chaos. On one side roaring and raking clumps of brush, soil, and debris was Big Brown. His eyes rolled wildly with anger. Steaming, slimy foam fell from his jaws as he tossed his head; his huge teeth were blood- stained, making pink foam.

On the other side, were a dozen troodons that darted forward while others flanked Big Brown, nipping and slashing. Their big, dagger-like claws made deep claw marks in Big Brown's pebbled skin, but his hide was so thick and tough that none of the cuts were lethal.

The pack roared back at the bigger animal. They were angry at being attacked in their territory and fearful of the bigger predator; their future had to be secured by winning the fight. Several of their kind lay on the ground, dead or dying.

The ones who were injured screeched but were ignored, were nipped at by their pack-mates, or were smashed as Big Brown stomped at them. The bigger dinosaur tried to mash the troodons into the ground, and he slashed at them as he stepped on them.

He knew they had to die and would be tasty.

Mattie screamed as a troodon leaped onto Big Brown, trying to bite his neck while the troodon's back legs frantically tore at his adversary. Big Brown swung to the side and sent the smaller creature flying through the air.

It landed close to Mattie, dazed from the fall, but its tiny brain was focused on Big Brown. The combination saved Mattie from being killed.

"Grab her; we have to run," Scott called to Harold. He doubted that would be easy to accomplish because Mattie walked closer, ducking behind the trees. She was acting foolish enough to get all of them killed.

"Jody," Mattie began to yell.

Harold slapped a hand over her mouth. "Stop it. He's gone. He ran away. Did you see him?"

She nodded. As Harold removed his hand, she whispered, "I saw him looking back, and he and Ricky, I think, ran, and a girl..."

"They have sense, then. Mattie, we have to go," said Scott as he prepared to hit her over the head and carry her if he had to. This was suicidal, and he was losing his temper. How could she risk their lives for a murderous son?

"Oh, no," Danny moaned as he knelt next to Scott, "that's Tommy."

Scott swallowed hard. He knew the teenager Tommy was almost truly feral. He understood and accepted that Jody's followers and the entire group engaged in cannibalism and had raped and killed Lori. He hated them for that. It didn't make it easier to stomach the sight of the young man, lying in the mud and feces, as the creatures trudged on him.

The slimy mud of debris, soil, and blood caked the cuts and scratches that Tommy suffered. It also covered the stub of Tommy's torn arm and the remains of one of his legs. The boy's face was partially ripped away, and Scott wondered how Danny even recognized Tommy.

Scott also felt a renewed sense of anger at Mattie for subjecting them not only to being in danger, but also to seeing the dead humans.

Now that he really looked, Scott unfortunately was able to identify more remains. A leg, an arm, and part of a ribcage, and a hand that resembled a fat, pale spider lay near the mud, and in another place were a leg and some globs of flesh. The troodons stopped at times to gulp down quick bites of the meat from the young people they massacred, but never paused long since they were fighting the bigger creature.

Repulsed, Mari rubbed her face as she cried because she had known these other children well. She had run away from them, but she hadn't wanted them to be slaughtered. She saw what remained of a girl she had loved in ways she didn't quite understand, and the brutal visage shook Mari to the core. Her grief was instant, and she screamed, "Keri!" She stepped from behind a tree, wailing uncontrollably.

A second too late, Danny yanked her back to the trees, but the troodons saw them.

Half the pack continued to battle Big Brown, but several others roared and stalked closer, their heads bobbing like birds' heads as they sorted out what the new creatures were, ready to defend their territory from any beasts that threatened them.

"Take Joy, and run," Scott ordered.

Tom began a protest, "Hey..."

"You are a liability to me. She is more of one. I said get out of here," Scott snarled. He saw words had the necessary effect; Tom and Joy ran. Scott hoped that Tom understood he had to say that to save Joy and Tom; it was likely Scott would die and be unable to explain later.

"Mattie, you and the rest get out of here," Alex said, "and as soon as you can." Probably, the order was a little premature because so far, there wasn't a clear way for her to get away. Harold, Danny, Mari, and Mattie were far too close to the troodons, and if Alex and Scott moved too fast, the movement would set off a frenzy of killing.

"Mari. We have to get *her*," said Danny as he held back, willing her to back-step to safety or at least to move back to where he was.

Before they could do anything, one of the largest troodons, a feisty, bad-tempered, hungry female, pregnant and in need of protein, came at Mari, raising her clawed left foot high and slashing forward. Mari made a tiny noise of fear and tried to twist around to run.

The claw cut Mari so cleanly that she only felt a faint stinging before she felt a terrible tugging sensation at her stomach; her belly spread wide open, and her guts slithered to the ground in a red-and-grey steaming mess. Mari stared at the mess with a sort of puzzled curiosity.

Danny stepped back so fast and hard that he ran into Mattie. They both fell.

Scott and Alex shoved forward with spears and knives, but they couldn't hold all the troodons back.

One animal lunged at Danny and eviscerated the young man, as it ripped out his throat with its big teeth. It gulped the hot blood.

The other creature knocked away Harold's weapons with its muscular neck and swung back again, grabbing Harold's head. The troodon's hunting partner began feeding on Harold's stomach as the man screamed in pain. A tug of war began and ended as Harold's head ripped from his body; each dinosaur ran away, taking part of Harold. Mattie shrieked.

"Get out of here. Run," Alex yelled at Mattie.

Scott and he saw Mattie look the way Jody ran, still considering following him, and it infuriated both men. It was as if Harold's brutal death was secondary.

Mattie listened this time and took off running down the trail. She was told to run, but Alex felt a faint wave of disappointment that she was so selfish not to help them fight.

Alex and Scott scored hits as they stabbed the troodons. Scott had to yell over the noise that the animals were making to shout, "Alex, follow them."

"No, you follow them. I have this," said Alex. He couldn't leave his best friend to fight alone; he was no coward.

Scott ducked and rolled to avoid a deadly back claw. When he got back to his feet, he realized he had lost his knife and spear and was helpless. A large male troodon came at him, roaring. Scott knew that he was about to die and dimly wondered if he'd come back in another shipwreck, if Helen and Littleton would get together, and if his group would ever make it back to their beach.

Two events saved Scott's life.

Big Brown was far too curious for his own good, and he turned to see why the humans were screaming.

Always opportunists, two of the troodons jumped a split second one after another; one slashed the beginning of a deep cut into Big Brown's throat, and the second's aim was so perfect that his claw opened the massive vein that lay a fraction deeper. Their teamwork was successful.

Once cut, the vein pumped furiously. Big Brown leaned over dizzily, and then thumped to the ground with a mighty bang, scaring and exciting the troodon pack. The entire pack ran to feed and enjoy the victory.

All of this occurred as Mattie ran away and was part of the reason Scott was still alive.

Had Scott still held his spear, he would have been saved, but the death of Big Brown was only part of Scott's salvation. It also caused all to leave except the one that would most assuredly rip out Scott's guts. However, the second event occurred, and that made all the difference for Scott.

"You're the best friend I have ever had. Thank you," Alex called. He steeled himself and walked right at the last troodon, hoping he would be proven wrong, and that he would survive. He hoped at the least that his death would be painless, but doubted it. "Back away."

Scott knew that if he remained, Alex and he would die because the troodon was between him and his spear. To stay and die would be to trivialize the gift Alex was extending. "Alex..." Scott didn't know what to say.

"Die, you son of a bitch," Alex shoved his spear into the troodon, and his aim was true. He had the strength to press the spear deep into the beast's chest, but before the troodon died, it reached up and clawed, ripping apart Alex's belly with a noise like tape being yanked from a roll.

To Alex's shock, he felt little pain. He felt tired, and there was a tug at his stomach, but as he fell to the ground, his death was almost as painless as he had wished. The troodon collapsed beside him, and both labored for breath as they died.

Before the rest of the pack could come and devour him, Alex died quietly, something seldom allowed on the island. He had a chance to reflect. He was always the smart person, yet never the hero, but he finally had a chance to be both.

"Give 'em hell, Scott," Alex muttered. He felt proud of himself and wished the best for his friends; he only wished he could have lived and been a hero. "Heroes die."

And he was gone.

Chapter 20: Off the Deep End

Scott stopped behind some trees that grew close together and would hide him. He pretended that he needed to catch his breath in the humidity of the jungle.

In reality, Scott had to stop because he was heaving as he cried aloud. He had suffered loss after loss, but none had caused him to cry this hard.

In a few minutes, he was able to walk again and follow the trail toward the beach, refusing to look back at what the monsters did to his friend's body.

"Scott!" Tom was relieved and pale with worry.

"Did Harold…" Mattie began. She changed her question and said, "Danny and Mari didn't make it."

Scott took a deep breath, but it didn't calm his temper or emotional pain. He thought of how Mattie had run off into the trees, trying to find her cannibalistic son and how she had called his name after they found the site of the dinosaur battle.

It didn't take him but a half a second to assign blame for everything. He ignored Tom and Joy for a few seconds and slammed into Mattie, yanking her almost off her feet by her shirt collar.

She yipped with shock and fear.

"You, stupid bitch. You caused Harold to die. You caused Danny and Mari to die, and you stupid, stupid whore, you caused Alex to get his guts fucking ripped out." He yelled so loudly that spit speckled her cheeks.

Joy burst into tears, for she assumed the worst, but hearing Scott say that, made her feel sick. She reached to hug Tom, but he stepped over to Scott and Mattie.

"I'm sick. I feel horrible. Amanda and Jade and many more died when they saved Amy and tried to save each other. Air Marshal Lynn died trying," Tom said softly.

Scott listened to Tom, stopping short of striking Mattie.

Tom continued, "When Fish died for me, I felt so guilty. I couldn't believe I was worthy of such a good man giving his life for me. Scott, it hurt so much. You and I know that Alex was smart and a good friend. Who is smarter than Alex is? None of us. Right?"

"Yeah," answered Scott.

"He knew what he was doing, didn't he? Did he give his life to save you?" asked Tom.

"Yeah," Scott said.

"I figured that Alex did it for a reason. Fish saved me for a reason. You can't blame Mattie," Tom said.

"That's not right. It's her fault. Hers and that cannibal kid of hers." Scott nodded to himself. "I won't hurt her. Relax, but you know what? I'm gonna kill Jody and bring his head to Mattie as a gift. How's that for payback, Mattie?" Scott cried so hard he could hardly see Mattie's face.

"Scott…" said Mattie.

"Shut up. Don't even look at me. Don't try to talk me out of it, either. I'll show you what getting Alex killed causes; I'll *show you*," Scott said as he stepped away from Mattie, letting her fall at his feet as she sobbed. He gave Tom a hard look and dared his friend to ask for anything more.

Tom didn't want anything else; he only wanted to stop Scott from killing Mattie outright. It was for his friend, not for her.

Tom felt like bawling a week solid for Alex. Heartsick over the loss of Alex, he blamed Mattie somewhat. Like Scott, Tom felt he needed someone to blame, and Mattie was responsible for this as far as Tom could tell.

Mattie looked at Tom for sympathy, but he averted her eyes.

She tried to get Joy to feel some measure of empathy for her position. Surely, another woman would understand and feel a little sorry for her; instead, Joy narrowed her eyes and muttered, "Bitch, I hope you die and they eat you."

"The dinosaurs?" Tom asked, not meaning anything, only filling in after Joy's vehement statement. To his shock, Joy was as cold and cruel as ever.

Joy pursed her lips and answered, "No, I hope her own son roasts her ass and eats her. She deserves it."

Scott began walking down the beach, laughing crazily. "I swear I like you again, Joy. You have truly reached your potential. Oh, Mattie, please run afoul of Joy. Please do. Fact is, I think she'd trip your ass right into a troodon."

He laughed for a half hour, amused with his own joke.

Chapter 21: Home at Last

The group rose early in the morning and broke camp, walked all day, and made camp again late in the day. While they made good time going back to their camp, it was miserable for them, as Scott pushed them to get back. He had no interest in anything on the island anymore. He only walked.

He considered that there had been six of them in his group, and then eight, and now four. Of all of them, Alex shouldn't have been the one whom they lost. Scott didn't know his curiosity would end in losing his best friend, and the guilt weighed him down.

While he had solved some mysteries as he had wished, the price wasn't supposed to be Alex; in a way it balanced, though. In gaining knowledge, Scott lost the one person who best explained the information gathered.

What a miserable balance.

One day as Mattie saw a small group of tiny bird-like creatures, she asked, "I wonder what that is?"

Scott responded with acid in his voice, "We'd ask Alex, but you got him killed." Scott glared at Mattie, wishing she had died.

She walked robotically and didn't say anything else unless specifically asked. At times, Mattie wasn't sure why she didn't go drown herself, but she still secretly wished to find her son, even if she didn't dare say it.

In some ways, she feared Jody and thought it would be best never to find him, especially since everyone wanted him dead. Mattie couldn't forget the maniacal look in her son's eyes when last she saw him; he hadn't looked like the boy she raised.

As they reached the garden within the walls of boulders, Scott agreed to spend two nights, not because of what anyone else wanted, but because he wanted to stay and remember Alex and how his friend had enjoyed all the food. The good food, the rest, or time itself was like a balm, and Scott found that he was less angry. He hated Mattie and still blamed her, but he didn't feel a need to hurt her or verbally assault her any longer.

Tom and Joy relaxed a little, ate fruit and nuts, and remembered stories about Alex that they shared. Scott even smiled a few times.

The next day when approached by a compsognathus pack, Scott slaughtered all he could. He took some of the cooked meat and ate it that night but left the bodies to rot and draw predators. He didn't care about what was right or wrong. He fashioned a new spear and carried it, always ready for a fight.

Tom cried himself almost sick when they returned to the site where the giant bones lay, knowing that Alex and Benny had loved that place and enjoyed seeing the old bones and forming theories about the dinosaurs and the island.

Joy was attentive and loving, but Tom drew further within himself, sinking into a depression that Scott understood too well. It was a delayed reaction.

It was with a sense of relief and a lot of guilt, interest, and humility that they returned to the shipwreck of the *Connie Louise*.

Months had passed since they left, and they had expected there would be a few differences, but what they saw was very altered.

Parts of the yacht were missing, and what was left was battered and now made a poor shelter. It looked half the size it was before, and woven palm leaves now covered the gaping holes.

Scott felt that the storms had hit the beach with a terrible intensity while the sea battered the yacht, yet it did not burn. While they shivered in the cold caves, the winds assaulted the group on the beach.

Stu faced Scott's group as they returned, watching with squinted, older-looking eyes, and Tyrese stood beside him. Tyrese smiled happily, but his smile wavered as he counted those who returned.

Scott saw many new people that he wondered about; however, Tyrese seemed at ease with them. The new people wore sun-bleached camouflage and looked formidable; they carried spears at the ready.

Tyrese said something, and the new people went back to their chores, still curious, but not alarmed. He was disappointed that

Alex wasn't with the group, and his shoulders drooped since he knew Alex wasn't going to return.

Benny ran to meet Scott, his eyes bright and darting. He didn't understand, yet. "Where's Alex? Is he coming later?"

"He didn't make it," Tom said.

"He…what? He didn't? That's…" Benny didn't finish.

"We know. It is." Tom understood what Benny couldn't put into words.

"I'm going to have to depend on you more, Benny. You just became the dinosaur expert. I hope you can fill a big role in helping us understand the dinosaurs," Scott said gently. He knew Benny admired Alex greatly, and he was able to muster the graciousness to let the boy down easily, but also made it clear that Benny would be needed far more.

"Benny can help," Tyrese said, "and he already helps with all kinds of stuff. He's grown up a lot lately."

"I can tell," Scott said, "and I'll need you, Benny."

"Sure, I can try," said Benny as he frowned, and with his face troubled, he walked back into camp to sit down. He had questions that he didn't want answers to, and he felt a dreadful ache in his throat as tears threatened. Seeing Scott's face made him know he wasn't alone in the grief.

Scott shook hands with Stu and Tyrese and then with Joe and nodded to the rest. Littleton stayed to the side and stared at Scott but didn't greet him or the others. Littleton shifted his eyes back and forth between Scott and Tyrese.

Scott felt something was terribly wrong. He looked around and noted the new faces again, but he also wondered if some more were inside the wreck and didn't know that he had returned. He went over the names and faces of those whom he missed seeing. Of all, three stood out.

"Stu, where is Kelly, and where is Helen?"

"You need to come in and drink some water, and we'll tell you," Tyrese said.

"Helen?" Scott called.

Tyrese laid a hand on Scott's shoulder and said, "Hey, we'll explain, but it was earlier, maybe two hours ago. We waited for you because Davey kept saying he knew all of you were coming back and would be here in a few hours. We waited. We had to."

Scott asked, "Where is Helen? Amy and Kelly?" He repeated himself. He realized that Benny had already looked upset before he saw Alex was missing. *What had happened?*

"Scott, Jody and Ricky…"

"What did they do?" Scott's voice rose. Mattie skittered away as if fearful he might harm her for being Jody's mother. She dreaded hearing the answer. "What in the hell have they done now?"

"They attacked a group at the spring. They got Helen, Amy, and Kelly. They stole them away. They have them," said Tyrese, trying to remain calm, but his eyes looked panicked.

Mattie expected a tirade. Tom was afraid Scott would kill Mattie, and Joy was kind of excited to think Scott was about to snap Mattie's neck. Instead, Scott threw his head back and laughed crazily again.

"Scott? Are you…" Tyrese didn't know what to think.

"Insane. I'm crazy. Who else *would* it be? Huh? Who else *could* it be? It's always him! *Always* Jody."

Stu hissed, "I wanna kill him." He knew Scott always tried to keep the peace and never wanted to hear that.

To Stu's shock, Scott stopped laughing and wiped his face as he grinned and said, "Really? I'm in. I intend to make him suffer a long time. Can you *handle* that?"

Stu grinned back and said, "Just watch me."

Chapter 22: Home Camp While Scott's Group Was Away

"Stop moping. If you keep it up, I'm going to get depressed," Kelly told Helen. She hated seeing the sadness when she had more on her mind than Helen's drama.

"I want Scott back. I can't help it. I'm worried."

Kelly glared at Helen and said, "I've been worried. The last few weeks...yesterday..."

The day before, everything was perfectly normal or as normal as life ever was on the island, and everyone was busy with chores and actually in good spirits. The only negative issues over the past few weeks were Helen's gloominess and Tyrese's commentary that he missed Scott and that he realized Scott was far more of a leader and they needed to accept that.

"Please stop, Ty," Kelly begged again.

"*If* he comes back, he may get eaten," Vera remarked. She sneered.

A small issue had happened several days before when Vera teased Amy about something, and Helen had snapped at her. The issue was insignificant, and both Helen and Amy had forgotten the incidence; Vera held a grudge as she always did.

Helen yelled at Vera, again telling her to shut up and act right, and that set off a vicious chain of events. Helen was particularly loud and verbally tough on Vera as she waved her arms and berated the girl. With no father left to keep Vera in check, her mother still injured, and Tom gone, Vera ran wild. Stu and Vaughn mostly ignored her behavior, causing her to act out for more attention.

Vera lost her balance when her once-wounded leg gave out on her and she fell onto the sand. She wasn't hurt, but as she fell, she landed partially on her little bird-like dinosaur, Angus, and broke his leg.

"Is he okay? I'm sorry, Vera," Helen backed down.

"Leave us alone," Vera yelled. She believed he could be healed and said she intended to nurse Angus back to health; she was furious with Helen for causing the situation.

Stu hated the sound of the little animal crying and squealing in pain for hours and threatened to break Angus' neck and end the chaos. That made Vera and Stu argue.

"He's a stupid animal," Stu shouted.

"So are you! Kiss my ass," Vera told her brother. She scooped Angus up and went down the beach to sulk.

Benny wondered about the little creature and attempted to talk to Vera about Angus, but she always waved him away and harangued Benny until he gave up.

Angus was a baby, making him cute, but like a baby, he also liked being well fed with treats. He would have grown up with Vera, but what would have happened when he reached puberty and his adulthood was unknown. Right now, he was an injured baby, and he made plenty of noise that carried into the trees.

A mother velociraptor heard his cries of pain and reacted, following the sounds to the beach. Angus wasn't her baby, but her instinct made her think of him as *hers*. Her pack came with her.

The very small pack contained only six creatures, and she was the alpha. All she knew was that the sounds came from one of her species that was crying with pain, and like any mother, she was highly aggressive and protective. She ran to the baby to claw and snap at Vera's face, trying to get the baby free; she thought Vera was harming it.

They protected the babies because those kept their species going. The alpha's attack was lightning fast and brutal.

Davey, Tyrese, and Stu ran to the velociraptors that were attacking Vera and slashed at them, clubbed them, and stabbed them with spears. The fight was over quickly, and the entire pack died as their blood stained the sand bright red. Stu stomped a foot down on Angus' skull, not caring what Vera thought.

Benny pointed and yelled, "I knew Angus was a bad sort of dinosaur. He was a raptor. A baby raptor."

"He's a dead raptor now," Stu said, wiping his boot on a log.

"I tried to tell her," Benny insisted.

"Vera never listens," Stu told Benny.

Kelly and Helen grabbed Vera and carried her to the fire to lie down so they could examine her wounds. Vera's face and hair were literally stripped away as if she had been scalped, and she had been cut deeply in several other places. She was left with bloody stumps where fingers once were. Kelly succeeded in cleaning a few of the gashes, but she couldn't stand Vera's screaming as she tried to clean the mess from Vera's face, her skull showing in patches all overhead.

"I need to clean the wounds, but she screams so much," Kelly said. She sullenly told everyone that she was trying to help Vera, but Vera's injuries were severe. Connie weakly tended her daughter, mostly crying over her and being of little medical help.

Later, Kelly shared the medical problems with Stu as she had many times before. She explained how she tried to help and had done all she could think of. She made her skills seem both miraculous and ineffective at the same time, belittling herself for her failures. She tearfully asked him what he would do.

In the morning, Vera was dead, smothered in her sleep during the night. They buried her at sea, as they had many others. Kelly squeezed Stu's hand but didn't say a word. He stoically comforted Vaughn and his mother and avoided looking at Kelly for several hours.

Kelly did her job.

Stu did his job.

They had different roles, and all anyone could do was his best. Each had to do what seemed best for the group. At least Vera wasn't screaming anymore.

Kelly worked harder than ever and made Helen change her attitude through sheer determination and a lot of tough talking. There was no place for depression in the camp, and they had jobs to accomplish.

Joe went back to creative cooking and taught Davey a lot. Davey also learned all Kelly could teach him, and he practiced with his spear constantly when he wasn't working on building muscles the old-fashioned way, not with the steroid-rich water. He was always there with Tyrese or Stu, ready to fight if they were threatened.

One day, Davey, feeling that Littleton was trying to get too close to Helen and feeling loyal to Scott, issued a few veiled threats, and to his shock, Littleton backed off, worried. Davey was pleased he had worked himself into a warrior.

"You been in the bad water?" Tyrese asked.

"Me? No way. Why? I know better," said Davey.

Tyrese looked flummoxed and said, "Davey, you have gotten buff. Do you not see it? Hell, you're almost as big as me and Stu."

"I am," Davey asked, "and imagine that. I've been working out; that's all, Ty. With Scott gone, I sure don't want you to fight alone. I've got your back."

Tyrese smiled and said, "That's good. You sure aren't the same man you were before. You're bad ass, man."

Davey grinned for an hour after that and never hesitated to help the other men. He had found his place; it wasn't as a silly stoner. He was a fighter.

The storms came, and they were fierce. For weeks, the group had to stay in the wreckage and eat smoked meat and canned foods while they whined and complained about being cooped up. Each longed for the sunshine and activities.

"I wonder if Scott and the rest found shelter?" Helen asked.

"I hope they did. Hey, the rains won't last forever, right?" Davey said.

Days later as the wind continued to hammer at the wreck and the rain continually came down in sheets, they wondered if the storms *would* last forever. When the skies turned yellow, a sense of dread overcame the group, and they huddled deeper within their damp blankets.

Waves began to batter the wreckage, and several of the massive waves dislodged part of the yacht. With the wind's help, the waves broke part of the yacht away and swept it out to sea.

Kelly was a little relieved because the part swept away was where Connie was, still being tended in Kelly's medical area.

Connie's wounds had started healing well, but then they became infected about the same time Vera died. Connie would have been fine after she fought down the mild infection, but her depression over Vera and her constant whining and complaining, along with Connie's insufferable demands, wore on Kelly's nerves. She had already hinted to Stu that Connie was causing the group to feel peevish and to act out.

Stu hadn't done anything yet, and Kelly never pushed, but she had hoped he would deal with his mother. Kelly knew that it was a touchy issue. She wasn't sure what she wished for Stu to do, but anything was better than nothing.

The waves sucked the section of wreckage into its clutches, swept it far out to sea, and dropped it to the bottom. Evidently, Connie went with it. At least she went quietly, or her screams were lost in the wailing winds. That was what everyone said and what Kelly decided had happened; if it were anything else, she didn't want to know.

The storms continued.

Davey watched Kelly, and she felt his eyes on her often. "Stop staring at me all the time," she said.

"I'm only learning what to do from you in case I ever have to help with anything medical. I have before, you know," Davey replied.

"There's nothing I'm teaching."

Davey shrugged as he said, "That doesn't mean I don't learn."

More parts of the yacht washed away, and holes appeared, allowing water to drip inside their home. They had to sleep and live closer. Slowly, the home that they felt was secure fell apart. It was another betrayal from the island.

"Maybe this place will stay together a few more days. Maybe the storms will stop," Tyrese said.

"Too many maybes in that sentence," Helen said, "and Scott is out there in this."

Tyrese nodded and said, "The storms may be lighter where he is, or maybe he found a good shelter. At least right now, as miserable as we are, we aren't in the jungle, huh? I doubt he is, either."

Helen jumped and asked, "Did you hear that?"

"I couldn't miss it. There's no telling what the storms are bringing in this time," Tyrese said.

Some days, the storms became wailing banshees that terrified the survivors with the howling wind, gigantic waves, and driving rain.

Other days, the skies were grey, and the rain was mist that never let up. Because the wood was wet, there was no way to make and maintain a cooking fire, so the bland food came from cans.

A few sunny days came some weeks after the storms had begun, enabling the group to set about reestablishing the camp and getting a fire going. Everyone saw the newcomers not long afterwards. The new people said they saw the smoke and followed it to the camp.

"People," said Helen.

Helen looked at the newcomers and back at Tyrese. "They're a mess, but they don't look as if they've been here very long."

"You think the storms wrecked them?" asked Tyrese.

"Yeah, why doesn't that really surprise me any longer?" asked Helen.

"I know," Tyrese admitted, "hello, welcome to the island, and no, there is no help coming for you or even for us."

"We figured that," a man said who was the commanding officer, a sergeant, in the Marine Corps. He shook hands all around and said, "I'm sorry if us coming here made you think help had arrived for you."

"I don't have hope anymore," Helen said honestly. "Besides, we could tell you looked less like help and more like survivors of some wreck."

"Exactly," Sergeant White said. He explained that they had suffered a terrible shipwreck that swept them almost to the tree line a few days' walk down the beach. "Luckily for us, it was the day the storms ended because we lost everything. People. Equipment. We washed up with nothing except our lives. The ship is gone."

"We have to explain about the creatures here…" Helen began.

Sergeant White nodded calmly and said, "We've seen them and have dealt with a few as well. Dinosaurs, aren't they? We were pretty shocked to see those bastards."

Sergeant White had lost a few people to the dinosaurs' first attack on them and more of his platoon to the sea and wreckage, but he was pragmatic and accepted what he saw. He said they ate what they killed and had little more than the meat and a fire. "We'd like to join you."

"It's very possible," Tyrese said. He wanted to learn more about these people before he invited them to be a part of the camp, "We lost one of our people and half of the wreckage we live in."

"It's better than we have," Sarg said.

Something about the way they were dressed looked different even if most were dressed in their fatigues. None of the people had guns, and even a few were dressed in civilian clothing.

Benny studied them closely and asked one of the women how she was a Marine and had blue hair at the same time. He figured she was one of the Marines because she was dressed like Sarg.

Her name was Rita, and she smiled a little, saying that the Corps allowed the blue hair as long as they were dressed correctly in their uniforms. She said she had lost her girlfriend in the wreck and took out her anger on the dinosaurs. "I love combat."

Benny's jaw dropped as he said, "I don't mean to be rude, but you are allowed to be openly gay? And women are in combat? Since when?"

"Sure, and since the last few years," Rita said.

Benny asked her the date. The adults around him watched him as if he were crazy for asking a foolish question, so he knew something was very strange.

It came as no real surprise that they were from a time thirty years in the future for most, and thirty-five years ahead of Benny's group. The island had dropped the future onto the sand.

"I can accept that we crashed and that there are dinosaurs. I see them, but you want me to accept that we are from another time? Like *Twilight Zone* stuff?" Rita asked.

"I can't make you believe it, but then I didn't believe these people immediately when they said I was from their past. They knew my boat, the *Violet Marie*," said Benny.

"The *Violet Marie?* What was your yacht?" one of the women, Susan, asked Tyrese.

Tyrese tilted his head and answered, "The *Connie Louise*."

Susan looked shocked. "I know them both. My, God, *you* vanished. You're part of why we are on our mission. My studies are in maritime losses. We are out here…there…wherever…to find out what happened to people like you."

"You knew we were lost?" Tyrese asked.

"Yes, we did. I'm sorry, but all of you have been declared: presumed dead, but no one knew how or why."

Tyrese grimaced and said, "Now, you know where we are, but you won't find out why or how we are here. Same as you. Why and how did you get here? A big, yellow-colored storm. No answers. Same as us."

Susan looked at Rita and Sarg, bewildered but fascinated as well. She knew their story, but not how it ended. Knowing that this was the remains of the *Connie Louise* didn't help at all in understanding.

Stu talked and explained their theories and experiences, feeling like someone in Littleton's group must have felt when speaking to someone in his own future. He explained well with help from the rest, and the new group listened, asked questions, and finally nodded.

"Well, okay," said Sergeant White.

"You aren't upset, Sergeant White?" Benny asked, interested in this new type of reaction.

"We don't like it. If there's a way home, I hope we find it, but no mission is a hundred percent okay. We know any mission may be the one that we never return home from. It's shit, but we accept the shit," Sarg said as he sighed. "Our mission was to protect the scientists, historians, and theorists, but we failed. The ship went down."

"You couldn't control that," Susan said.

"Why were you looking for us this long after we went missing?" Tyrese asked.

"We aren't the first to look. Many looked for you. You aren't the only boat or aircraft to go missing. For years, people have searched and wondered. It looks like we're the ones to find you."

Tyrese smiled at the sergeant. "Fat lot that does, right? Welcome anyway. Sorry, we have little to offer you."

Benny listened to them talk. Sarg was tough looking, polite, and likable, and so were his men: Trent, Jered, and a man they called Iowa. Rita was funny and buff and was like one of the men except for her short blue hair. Jana was a medic and a civilian, and she, Davey, and Kelly immediately began to talk about medicine as they told her about the steroid water and injuries they had treated.

Susan was a quiet, young woman, younger than the others, and she and Vaughn made friends fast. For the first time, Vaughn relaxed, let go of his emotional pain, and enjoyed talking to someone and laughing again.

Shannon was as tough as Sarg and the others, and as strong and tall as Tyrese, pretty in a classical African Princess way, and a Marine. She made friends with Tyrese and Davey as they talked about working out and maintaining a muscular physique. Davey was proud to be included.

A scientist with them named Michael, was louder and more opinionated than the rest. He wasn't good with social cues, and most began to avoid him or roll their eyes as he lectured and tried to tell everyone what each was doing wrong. Even though he was similar to Stu, he and Stu didn't hit it off, and Michael stayed alone, studying various plants.

Jerry was the final member of the group, and he interviewed everyone about any experiences. He was not only interested in his research but also practiced with spears and worked out with the rest.

More strong people available meant they would be able to repair a little of their camp. The beach was altered, and an enormous amount of clean up was required. Brush, leaves, and small branches littered the sand, along with two large uprooted trees tossed across the beach. As the trees dried out, some of the men cut them for firewood.

Tyrese suggested that a tree probably was carried by the wind and slammed into part of the yacht, breaking it away. Deep holes made him also assume that more trees had been washed out to sea with the storms. The tree line looked different, and so did the yacht and sand around it. Their beach had increased because of the missing trees, but the area from the wreck of the yacht to the water had decreased. Had there been much more of the stormy conditions, no yacht would be left, and most of the group would be dead.

"You've done well here. Good leadership," Sarg said one day.

"Thanks," Tyrese and Stu said as they looked at one another.

"I'm not one to give you orders even though I lead a platoon, but I can give you some advice. Seems to me you've done well with what you have going on here."

"We do at times," Tyrese said. He was glad the others had arrived in time to help with the camp. It made him feel safer to have the military around, too. Sarg was helpful, but never tried to take over, and only made suggestions at times.

Sarg went on, "Maybe that's been a lot of luck, too. What I'm saying is that at some point, you may wish you had a definite leader. Frankly, me and my team would like to know who we're reporting to."

"Is this how you start taking over?" Stu asked.

Michael chuckled, but his Sergeant gave him a hard look. "That's not what I said at all. I said what I meant."

"I don't think we *ever* voted," Kelly said. She gave Stu a slight nod and said, "You and Scott decided."

Helen frowned and then exploded, "I saw that little nod. Why would we vote when *we* were the ones who went out to get water each time and had to fight for every supply we had? We picked Tyrese."

"*You* did. He's an easy choice since Scott can ramrod the leadership," Stu said.

"I pull my weight. Are you a nurse? No. That's *all* me," Kelly went red-faced. She was tired of Helen's opinions. Kelly valued those who benefitted the group, and Helen paled in Kelly's view.

"That's not fair, Stu," Tyrese complained.

"Now, I have my answer," Sarg said. "What I get from this is that I need to report to Scott. If he comes back."

Tyrese narrowed his eyes and sighed, "Sarg is right. Scott tried to get me to lead, but Scott has been making the tough choices. He stepped up far more often than I ever have. He's a better leader."

"But we didn't vote for him," Kelly said.

Shannon smiled and said, "And we know whom to go to in the meanwhile. *Tyrese*. Sarg is good at figuring things out."

"You don't know everything. You act so smug, but you have no idea what we've been through: Fish died, and so did Amanda, Durango, and some of the rest, and even Tom's arm had to be removed."

Helen huffed, "And *you* weren't there when we had to fight troodons and Utahraptors time after time or when the slugs attacked us. Also, you weren't there when Lori was murdered. I've been there for every dinosaur battle."

"And?" Kelly's eyes glittered.

Sarg and Shannon backed off and looked surprised at the hidden emotions that were coming out. Sarg had wanted to discover one bit of information but had seemingly broken into a hornet's nest he didn't know even existed.

Days passed, and the tension tempered.

Helen and Davey and sometimes, Tyrese, often stared off across the beach, wondering if Scott and the rest would return and when. They wondered how long to wait before they gave up. Helen felt eyes on her and turned to see Littleton watching her.

"Why are you staring at me?"

"I was just looking to see if well…it's been weeks now."

"And?"

"Helen, I like them. Tom is funny and easy going. Alex is smart. Scott is…well…Scott, but I think they aren't coming back."

"What does that mean? What is '*Scott is Scott*'? And how can you say they have deserted us?" Helen felt her temper flaring, aware of all the reasons she was so upset but unwilling to talk to Littleton about her reasons.

"I didn't say they deserted us, Helen," he tried to be gentle with his words. "We know how much danger there is out there. Scott and Alex don't have much back up. I just think we have to be realistic."

"You just don't think at all. He *is* coming back."

Littleton shrugged and said, "Maybe. Until then, Benny and Amy are my responsibility, too. Even if Scott returns, I'll help with them."

Helen understood he cared about the teenagers and respected that. However, she hadn't missed the fact that he tried to initiate a family-like atmosphere with them that included her. She knew he tried to sit near her or do chores with her, and it made her feel petulant.

She also saw things that Littleton didn't see, or maybe he saw the same things as she, but didn't understand the relevance.

In the last few weeks, Benny trained with the Marines constantly, and he went with them frequently, as did Tyrese and Davey, to hunt for meat. He hadn't lost his boyish interest in the dinosaurs and loved to talk about theories and paleontology, but he was becoming a fighter as well, knowing he needed to survive if he still wanted to watch the beasts safely.

Amy took her mother's death hard and never forgot that Jada and Amanda had given their lives to save her. She had no love for Vera, but she was one of the few who cried when Vera died, upset to see someone her own age die.

While Amy was quieter and prettier than she was bright, she used all of her time to learn how Joe worked, helping him with the cooking, and she had a definite skill for preparing smoked meat under Joe's tutelage. Helen was immensely proud of her for also learning how to shape spear tips, by banging away at the stones to make sharp edges.

Both of the teens had learned important skills. Helen knew they were becoming self-sufficient, something Littleton was still lacking. Helen felt vile, obscene words about to come out of her lips and bit back a response. That he might be right about Scott dying out there away from camp was also infuriating and something Helen didn't want to hear.

She refused to speak to Littleton for days, not caring who noticed. Everyone snickered when he wasn't looking. Helen preferred to be with Amy and Benny or with Tyrese and Davey or with another female, Rita, who was funny, honest, and very positive.

Several times, Helen felt as if Davey wanted to tell her something, something so deep it might be his way of unburdening his conscience, and she tried to encourage him to share his thoughts, but he clammed up each time. Something nagged at him, and Helen knew he wanted to share with her for some reason but forced herself to wait until he could open up.

One morning, Davey said he saw smoke from far away, but when he tried to point it out, it was either gone or the wind was blowing it in a way so no one could see it any longer. He complained and swore he saw the smoke; no one tried to say he had imagined it, but as to whom the fire belonged, there was no way to know.

"I think it's Scott, and he's coming home," said Davey.

"What the *hell*? I need help," one of the soldiers yelled. It was the one called Iowa, and his face was battered and bloodied, and he struggled to run, despite wounds in his side and thigh that both bled badly down his leg, making it dark red and wet. Everyone liked him for his humor and bravery; he was easy-going and friendly, and seeing him wounded was horrible. Of all the soldiers, he was one of the toughest.

"Iowa! Damnit, Jana," said Sarg.

"I'm with you, Sarg," said Iowa as he ran behind the Sergeant, Shannon, and Trent. Jana noticed Iowa hadn't called for Kelly but then remembered that Kelly had been with Iowa in a group that went for water.

Tyrese and Davey ran toward the tree line. Nervous and scared, Davey was sure they hadn't heard any trampling, stomping, or roaring which usually indicated there was a pack hunting near the closest water source that the group used for clean drinking and cooking. It wasn't very far and had been safe to use for weeks. Even when predators came around, they didn't stay long after Benny taught the group to use urine-marked mud to keep a perimeter around the spring safe from most nosy beasts.

"What's going on, Iowa. I need your status ASAP," Sarg said. "Talk to me, man." He watched Jana apply pressure to Iowa's wounds and needed to know what was going on before his soldier passed out from shock. Like the rest, Sarg was perplexed because he had not heard any loud noises. While he awaited Iowa's report, he watched and listened for anything indicating a pack was attacking them.

Iowa and Rita and Jerry, one of the scientists on board the ship, Helen, Kelly, and Amy had been gathering water at the spring. It was a safe place to go, and Iowa and Rita were tough as old leather and dependable. Jerry was a bit of an egghead and talked about theoretical physics and biology with Benny and Susan until everyone else became bleary-eyed. While Jerry was an intellectual, he was a formidable fighter, having acclimated to the situation quickly.

Sarg couldn't imagine how any animals managed stealthily to attack his people. He couldn't have provided better security had he been at the spring himself. He knew his people were good.

"Awe, Sarg, they hit us hard. They killed Jerry right off before we knew what was going on. Rita is dead, sir. There's no way her head could pop like that and..."

"Who? What? What did this?"

"Not a what. It wasn't a dino. Not claws or teeth, Sarg," Jana said, "a spear, I think."

"Kids. Kids, but they had dead eyes," Iowa shivered and passed out.

Chapter 23: My Past or Your Future

This was the morning Scott and his group returned.

"You didn't do anything?" Scott demanded. He looked at the faces before him.

"We were about to, but first we had to get Iowa settled, and we couldn't let Rita and Jerry lie in the trees and get munched on." Sarg paused and held up a hand. "Yes, we searched for the women. We went after them; we think Jody and Ricky got them. They were just gone, but I think we can track them. Davey here said you were on the way."

"How could you wait a minute to go after them? How could you wait this long? You know what they'll do to Helen, Kelly, and Amy. You *know*," Scott said as he looked at Tyrese and then Sarg.

"I do know. I understand, and I assure you that we'll move fast and do everything we can to bring the women home and eliminate the enemy. There's more to us being here, and this unfortunate...well...piece of shit timing."

"I don't understand, Sergeant White," Scott said as he paced the camp and at any second was about to run into the trees to find Helen.

Stu paced as well, stopping only to curse.

The sergeant and his troops stayed alert, ready to grab anyone who tried to leave before the situation could be explained. The time for complete honesty was upon them, and ethically, there was a need to share it.

"I have to explain first."

"Then do it," Scott told Sarg. He didn't like that they were being kept from going after the women.

"I know it's as foreign for you to hear this as it was for Littleton to hear when he appeared five years into the future."

"Or all of them came back to my present time," Littleton said.

Sarg raised his eyebrows to show his point was made. "All of you are either my past, or I'm your future. It hardly matters here, does it?"

"I wish Alex were here," Scott said. "He understands this. *Understood* it."

Sarg spoke a long time, "The point is that it doesn't matter *here*. We're all in the same place at the same time. Susan and the rest have explained it, and we understand as best we can. Now, I need you to understand a few things. First, as you can see, a storm is rolling in. Usually they come in as a strong front, but if you look, well, Susan said that it's huge…"

"It's probably the biggest storm we have seen in this area. We've tracked hurricanes that didn't look this bad. It's moving slowly, but it's enormous. It's storm season here, yes, but that's one big storm that's coming," Susan said.

"And? We may be swept away, you mean? It might be better to go to the caves where Mattie's husband and the rest lived a while? Is that your plan?" Tyrese asked.

"Normally it would be," Susan admitted, "but there are a few other issues," she said as she sighed. Explaining, she told them something that her group had held back until they were sure about it. Even though the ship crashed and they lost their weapons, research, and the lives of many aboard, that didn't mean the mission was over with.

They had been on the sea to find out why more ships and planes were vanishing at the rate of almost a half dozen per year, counting only those they were sure couldn't be explained any other way. Several major airliners and a hand full of military planes and boats had disappeared, and Susan was part of the team assigned to discover the reason.

Tyrese blinked as he asked, "What *is* the reason?"

Susan looked shocked that she was asked that of all questions. "I…we…that's something we don't know. We know that the storms do some horrible things. Before we were sent out here, a boat had washed up on the coast of Florida. The results of that are confidential, but…"

"Was it us?" Scott asked.

"Or us?" Littleton asked.

"Me?" Mattie joined in.

"None of you," said Susan as she saw relief on their faces. She could only share that much, but it was what they were most concerned about. "It was the third anomaly. Until then, it had never happened, and then there were three instances of lost wrecks showing up. The yellow-looking storms occurred right before those three appeared. Look at this place. Doesn't it seem as if there were suddenly more wrecks here?"

"Storm season," said Tyrese.

Scott frowned at Tyrese. Maybe, but he wondered and tried to think as Alex would while he waited for a chance to run past the soldiers and get to Helen. He was like a caged animal.

He tilted his head with some curiosity. "It's happening more, and it's spreading, isn't it? The time loops? The *whatever* it is? That's why this was so important to you. Everyone...the higher-ups became worried. Those wrecks that showed up scared you, Sarg," said Scott.

Sergeant White nodded. "Exactly. Right before our ship went down, we got one more communication sent. It was to come get us only when we set off a homing beacon. We had to finish this mission. We thought that even if no one could rescue us in the storm we were in, we might could find something."

Tyrese's face lit up as he said, "You have a beacon? Can they find you? *Us*?"

Everyone began talking at once.

Stu grunted and said, "But if we return with you, it's to your time, right?"

No one had thought of that except for Susan and the other scientists and the soldiers.

She nodded and said, "We planned to wait and gather more research before setting off the beacon, but that storm you see rolling in, what if it's as bad as we expect? What if it tosses things here that are far worse? What if...well, I could go on."

"You set the beacon off?" Scott asked.

Sarg shrugged. "Yeah, we did. If there is anyone out there, we're going home. We have a specific amount of time."

"We're wasting it by not looking for Helen, Kelly, and Amy!" Stu thundered.

"Iowa knows where they're going. He heard enough to know. We can find them and get them back. We have to make sure all of you understand this. If anything goes bad, there is no waiting. Be here; there won't be another chance. We just hope they can get to us. We may be too late because of the storm."

"You can't come back?" Scott asked Sarg.

Benny piped up and said, "No, because if that storm alters anything, then we don't exist *here* or *there* or anywhere. We're invisible again, lost in a loop. That beacon is *just* for the time periods when we match up."

"We are only in the right time and place for a little while," Scott said. "Okay, then why are we wasting time *here*?"

"If we chase them and if Jody and Ricky kill the women, we will be sad and regret it, but we will think it would be over for them, right? Scott, if we cause those men to kill the women, then there is a possibility that they will come back in another scenario. They will return *here*. Again. They will relive this in a new way."

"That's why we can't meet ourselves. We have to die, don't we? Once dead, we can loop again, and if the scenario is just right, we land here," Benny added.

"That means you have to think. Before we go, you need to reconcile in your head that you may sentence them or yourselves to be stuck here, and to repeat the wreck they were in. Maybe. We don't *know*."

Stu looked at Scott, and they both grinned.

"What?" Sergeant White asked. He didn't understand the looks on the men's faces.

"Dude," Davey laughed, "you are slow. We never did expect to go home."

Chapter 24: On the Trail

Scott had time to think as they followed the animal path.

It had hurt when he denied Tyrese's coming along, but the people on the beach needed Tyrese with them to be a leader. He had to get them aboard a rescue ship, and he had to leave Scott's group if it came to that. He was dependable to do what was hard, painful, and right. Even if Sarg had left Trent in charge, they knew it was Tyrese who would make the difficult choices. Sarg knew that, too.

Also, there had been a hell of a fight between Joy, Stu, and Tom, as they decided on who would go on the rescue mission. It would have been amusing had it not cut into their time and resulted in a division of the survivors' group.

Mattie demanded to go even before Scott decided to drag her with him, and that part worked out fine, but it caused Stu to make several remarks that made Mattie's temper flare. Stu made no effort to conceal the fact that he was going to kill Jody.

Neither did Scott.

Stu said he wanted to make the feral pair pay for taking Kelly. That resulted in Tom agreeing that he wanted payback for Kelly, who was once his fiancée. Unfortunately, Tom's verb use was wrong, and instead of saying she *was* once his fiancée, he used the present tense *is*. Stu fired up over the wrong word choice, but while he started to curse and make snide remarks, Joy was the one who went ballistic first.

Stomping her foot, Joy demanded to know why Tom cared about rescuing Kelly so much now that Stu was with her. She said she might have slept with most of the men on the island, but she ended up with Tom and asked him if he were going to toss her aside. That remark made all of them snicker and avert their eyes. Even the newcomers hid smiles.

Tom flushed bright red. He yanked Joy to the side and whispered to her a few minutes after which she sulked back to the fire. He said he was going to rescue the women.

Scott wondered about that, considering Tom felt Kelly had used the removal of his arm as revenge, not to save Tom's life. Maybe Tom wanted to see her dead. It was something Scott couldn't be sure about.

Jana was along in case they needed medical help, and there were Sarg, Jered, Mattie, Tom, Stu, Scott, and Davey. As far as Scott could decide, there were two extra people they didn't need for this. They were there possibly todie, something he didn't like. Tom didn't need to be there, and neither did Davey.

Scott vetoed Davey's going but then changed his mind as Davey said something that made Scott pause.

"I have your back. *Trust* me."

Scott didn't know what that meant and didn't have time to ask, as Sarg got them moving at once, saying they had to make up all the time they had wasted.

Although Scott watched for anything unusual, nothing was wrong other than the odd feeling he had that there were several motives for those in the group. Few motives involved actually rescuing the women as the main objective.

"The wind is stronger. Feel that cool breeze?" Sarg asked.

"Yeah, I do. It's hot but not like it usually is," Scott said.

"Who is the female that Iowa said is with the feral kids?" Sarg asked.

"No clue. Mattie doesn't know who survived and who didn't. It could be any of the girls from her plane," Scott said.

"I don't know; did you see Mattie's face when Iowa told us a female was with the boys? She went pale, and her eyes looked hinky to me. You know her better than I do. Maybe she was just sad, remembering the little girls," Sarg remarked.

"Maybe. Did you ask her?"

"Sure, I did. Nothing. I dunno. You're the boss around here, but have you considered how the wild kids have always been a step ahead of you guys?"

"What are you saying?" Scott asked.

"I have no idea what anything means. I know it feels wrong, and then there's the other thing Iowa said before Jana gave him that pain shot. He, Jerry, and Rita went into high alert as soon as they saw the female with the boys. Your women didn't. He said they didn't look afraid."

"Maybe they were…you know…women are compassionate. They were concerned as soon as they saw the other girl," said Scott.

"Do you think Helen is that stupid, Scott? She's a sharp woman. Amy is young. Kelly is pretty sharp as well. They'd have been concerned. Maybe reactive," said Sarg.

"And?"

Sarg shrugged and said, "And nothing. I have nothing at all but the hinky feeling. It strikes me as off."

Scott digested that.

Sarg went ahead at the spring they had once used. They listened for predators, but the coming storm seemed to be causing most of the wildlife to start preparing to flee.

"Why'd you say that back there? About trust?" Scott asked Davey.

"I don't think we can trust Stu at all. Tom hasn't been the same since Fish died saving his life. He changed right that second," said Davey.

"Like with screwing Joy an hour later?"

Davey snickered and said, "Yeah. That. Seriously, that was *not* the Tom we knew, but I think it might have been okay because part of that was high fever. When Kelly took his arm, he went to a dark, paranoid place."

Scott told Davey in whispers what Tom had shared. "He doesn't trust her at all, but he's out here to save her. Weird."

"I think…*hope*…Tom is still good, but he may have other reasons for being here. He's right about Kelly. She and Stu think people don't see…" He gulped.

"See what?" asked Scott.

Davey knew time was short. Sarg was showing them which way to go, and it was in the direction of the old caves near where the Utahraptors hunted. This might be his last chance to ease his conscience and tell Scott something that could be vital.

"Remember in the cave with Shonna? You and Helen were all around it, but the deal was could I...you know...my hand...over her nose and mouth?" asked Davey.

"I remember," said Scott.

"I could. I did, but I didn't want to. I learned that from seeing someone else do things like that. Supposedly, it was merciful, but why would anyone's eyes light up when he had to do something that damned horrible? Why would anyone *like* doing that shit?"

Scott felt as if he had been punched. "Kelly?"

"Yup. And?"

"Stu. Oh my, God, Tom is right?"

"Probably, she's not who we thought, Scott. I don't think Tom means for either of them to...well...go home if anyone even could. I think he wants them to come back in a scenario. I saw the way his head jerked up and he smiled when the others explained all that to us. It was like a light went on in his head; I saw it."

Tom wanted another chance with Kelly, but with a Kelly who had never gone through the same experiences and who would never have removed his arm in a fit of fury. Maybe he had hopes for his brother as well.

"That's insane," Scott said.

"I won't argue with that. Thing is, Scott, I believe that Sarg knows all of this. He's smarter than you can imagine. I've watched and listened for weeks. He's brilliant, actually. I think Sarg knows exactly what he's offering, and he told us that and made us wait, so we knew. So *Tom* knew."

"Why?"

"Because this is his only chance. He gets to play God. Maybe because it's the only way Sarg knows to be fair," said Davey as he sealed his lips when Tom walked closer. They moved into the rocky area in silence as Sarg made a motion.

Scott had more to think about.

At the base of the rocks, Tom stopped and looked at a bone in the dirt, one that was mostly covered but that came loose when Tom worried it with his foot. It was many months old or older. It could have been from anything, but it was a human fibula.

"It could be from anyone. It could be much older or more recent," Scott said. Tom nodded and with help, he was able to start climbing the rocks.

Scott and Davey knew that Tom was remembering Fish who died for him right there. Maybe the bone belonged to Fish. Scott tried to ignore the possibility and watched Tom struggle to climb with only the one arm, but Jered helped him. Even with a limb missing, Tom climbed easier when he was not being chased by Utahraptors; Tom was able to plot his ascent and pick out handholds. Tom paused at the spot where Fish had helped him climb, and then he had fallen to his own death.

Scott wondered if the climb were easy for everyone because there were no rush and no threat, but the climb was easier even for him. He thought he was far stronger now than he had been then. No matter what it was, Scott was happy to find that the entire group had made it to the top. Wondering if Tom were suicidal and wanted it to be at this spot had crossed Scott's mind, but he wasn't, it seemed.

"I figured you'd push me off the top," Mattie said to Scott.

He narrowed his eyes and said, "The top goes on for a while." He wouldn't push her, but the idea to do it had crossed his mind.

"Just checking," said Mattie.

Sarg motioned them to be quiet again. He thought they were incapable of a stealthy mission. No wonder so many of their group died; they simply couldn't shut up. He motioned Scott to lead with him so they would know where they were headed. It might also cease the chatter.

At the edge of the cave, they waited.

Sarg was about to issue more orders when a voice called out, "Come on in. I guess it's time."

Sarg and Scott stepped nervously into the cave, leaving the rest behind. A warm fire made them aware of how chilly the wind had become. The cave was dry and warm, and someone had cleaned up inside, making everything feel cozier.

On a rock across the cave sat a young man. Moving around him was Amy who was nude and had bruises and was sporting a blackened eye and a split, puffy lip.

Amy looked at Scott and Sarg with little interest, but stayed at her task of brushing and sweeping dust away, scrubbing at a few of the stones to get them clean. Her eyes were dull, and she didn't seem to recognize the men who appeared. From her neck, a thick leash of hide ran from her collar to Jody's hand. He gave her a tug that sent her sprawling.

"Hey. We understand. No need to hurt her," Sarg said, keeping his hands raised. He held his spear but didn't advance. Jody's knife was glittering close to Amy.

"You tired of chasing me, old man? We've sure chased each other, huh?" asked Jody as he smiled.

"We have," Scott admitted. His throat almost seized as he saw Helen on the ground, huddled in a fetal position. A obvious knot on her forehead seeped blood. "Is she…"

"No, she's alive. For now. I plan to eat her, actually. She's not as good a mate since she is already pregnant," said Jody.

"Oh, man, you didn't know? How funny. Yeah, she's pregnant. Got a belly going already," said Jody as he grinned. "I aim to eat her and the baby. Yum."

Scott shook with anger.

Naked and with her wrists bound, Kelly lay close to Helen. She glared at Jody and didn't speak.

"She's alive. She'll make a good mate if I want a second. She was Ricky's but the damned sneak had a knife."

Ricky lay in the shadows. Scott and Sarg looked the way Jody glanced and saw that Kelly had managed a gut wound that had killed Ricky.

"Good for Kelly. You might as well let Amy go. This isn't going to end well for you, no matter what. I came to kill you," Scott said conversationally. He hoped he could save Amy, but no matter what, he planned to kill Jody.

"What does it matter? I'll come back, right? Oh, you didn't think I knew that? Man, I've seen plenty on this island. Probably more than you have. I think I can kill Amy and Helen before you can take me out. You aren't much. What's a military without the guns? Nothing," Jody said as he laughed.

"Don't," Scott warned Sarg and Jody. "How about a trade? I want Helen. For her, I will give you a gift." It was all Scott could think of.

"What trade?" asked Jody.

"Send in Mattie," Scott yelled.

Mattie walked into the cave, her eyes darting around. Before she could run to her son, Scott grabbed her arm and held her still. She called out to Jody.

He looked stunned. "I thought I imagined…they never told me…Mother? Mama?"

"Jody, sweetheart, Mama is here, now. I've looked for you for so long, but…"

"I saw you die. I…" His face was filled with pain. After she died, Jody hated the island, hated everyone who was alive, and enjoyed the chaos and misery that he immersed himself in. "You left me on my own."

"I didn't mean to. In my world, you left me."

"Trade, Jody?" Scott asked.

Mattie lunged at Scott, pushing him off balance, and as he fell, she yanked away and ran to Jody.

Sarg pulled his arm back, feeling he could accurately hit his target with his spear, but just as he started the forward motion of his arm to send the spear into Jody's chest, a weight hit him and began biting and scratching. Talons raked his throat, and a blade-like object slid into the heart.

Chapter 25: Beasts

Scott thought they had been attacked by velociraptors or small troodons, but the creature, which stabbed Sarg and began to lick at the blood, was neither of those species.

A tanned, naked woman crouched like an animal and lapped at the crimson gush. *Pam.* Scott sat back and took it all in as Mattie ran and hugged Jody and knelt at his feet.

Iowa said there was another female, but Scott assumed it was another one of the feral girls. Had Mattie guessed or seen her? Had she known? Maybe that was what she hid from them. How could they ever have guessed that Pam was alive after all this time? They thought she died at the spring, eaten by the ceratosaurs.

Pale scars crisscrossed her face where glass had cut her in the original wreck of the *Connie Louise*. Kelly's stitches were good, but they had scarred Pam further.

Months before, Scott thought Pam recovered well and had stopped being the spoiled, pretty elitist she was before the storm and the wreck. She was far more personable. Tyrese and the rest carried a heavy guilt over her supposed death.

"Pam is not the way you may remember her. Since your people left her to die and I saved her, she has been very *appreciative*," said Jody.

"That's kind of sickening," Scott spat.

"Yeah? You'll find it worse to know what her favorite meal is," Jody chuckled. "She is fully with us now. She was the one who got Helen, Amy, and Kelly to come to her. She sucked them right in."

"As bait," Scott said, "and Iowa said there was another female. It makes sense now. This doesn't change anything. I have people outside. You're still going to die, Jody."

"Am I? You have people outside? Out where Ricky and I left some freshly killed compys? Out there where I bet the *big ones* have figured out how to get to meat."

Scott heard a distant roar and realized he heard it seconds before, but thought it was the wind picking up. Before him was

Jody who might kill Amy, Helen, and Kelly at any second and Jody's crazy mother who might help him.

Beside Scott was Pam who was beginning to rip flesh from Sarg's face with her teeth; she was insane and carried a deadly sharp knife. Farther away, Utahraptors were coming to feast on Sarg's friends.

Scott didn't like the odds.

Jered broke the rule of silence. "Sarg? We have company out here," he yelled from outside the cave, making everyone glance that way. He didn't know his sergeant was already dead.

Mattie jumped away from Jody and took a small knife from the floor of the cave. Her eyes on Scott, she stabbed Kelly before Scott could say anything or move. Pam was ready with her knife, and Scott didn't dare try anything.

Kelly screamed.

With bloodstained teeth, Pam grinned and taunted Scott with her knife. She advanced on him, willing to fight it out.

One of them was about to die.

Pam suddenly whirled to the side, screaming as a spear went through her side and into her belly and out again. Davey, on the other end, kept pushing until she was pinned to the floor, dying. He dropped his end of the spear. Although he was saddened to see whom he had killed, he gave Scott a short nod, saying, "We have company."

"I heard."

With her rock, Mattie moved to stand over Helen as Jody yanked Amy closer to him. They still had hostages.

As Jered, Stu, Tom, and Jana ran into the cave to avoid the advancing Utahraptors, they slid to a stop. The creatures outside might stop and feed only on the bodies of the compys, but they also might try to get into the cave and come after live prey. The mouth of the cave had to be guarded. Davey and Jered turned to do that if needed.

Tom, Stu, and Jana went to Kelly.

Jody didn't bother to warn them away; he didn't care. He watched as Jana knelt and worked over Kelly. "I can save her. It's not too late. Come on, Kelly. Try for me. I need some help though."

Tom put his arm on Stu's chest and said, "No."

"What? That's Kelly. She needs help," responded Stu.

"Let her go," Tom said.

"You still want her after all this? Well, guess what you asshole, she picked me. Me! I finally bested you, Tom. I'm stronger, I have two arms to protect her, and I'm not with that whore, Joy," Stu spat as he yelled.

"You *are* stronger. She didn't chop off your arm, so yes, I give you that as well. I even give you the part about Joy being a whore, but she's done good by me. I'm okay with what Joy has done in the past. It isn't that," said Tom.

"Really? Tom, you hate Kelly so much you'd let her die? What happened? That's more like me than it is you."

"I don't hate her," Tom said. "This place...it's made all of us different. Look at Jody. Look at yourself. Look at me. Do you understand that there is a chance Kelly can come back in a wreck and be unblemished by all this? She could be pure and good again...not like she...you know what she's capable of."

Stu squinted, turned his head, trying to understand, and asked, "What?"

"You want to reset her personality? Tom, that's sick. You'd have to stay here and wait for that even if it happened. You could wait for years. Decades. Forever. It could happen across the island where you would never know," Davey said.

Tom didn't answer.

Stu laughed without humor as he said, "Oh, I get it, and then if it happens, she is yours, and I lose again."

"It isn't about you. It's about her," Tom said. "You go home, and I stay. It's simple."

"I need help," Jana said again.

Stu turned, and Tom head butted his brother in the stomach, and they both went down.

At the same time, Mattie reacted, running away from Helen and straight at Jody. She had dropped her little rock and now carried a large stone that she smacked him in the head with, knocking him to the side. Then, she hit him again.

Everyone stopped moving.

Tom and Stu stared at Mattie with disbelief on their faces.

Mattie sat down and leaned against Jody who breathed shallowly. She smiled tiredly and said, "So much to take in. Resetting? All I wanted was to find my sweet boy and raise him here or wherever. Who cares?"

"What?" Stu asked.

"Tom, thank you for saying that. It made sense to me and showed me the way to make this right. Jody and I are going to get another chance. I have faith in the next time."

"Mattie..." Davey began as he looked over his shoulder again.

Mattie ignored him and continued, "Back there down the other tunnel is a way out of here. I came here looking for my baby; anyway go. Those things are going to try to get in here, and you can't hold them off."

"What about..." asked Davey.

"I'll handle things here. I *am* his mother, after all," said Mattie.

"Kelly?" Tom asked.

Jana moved away from Kelly and was leaning over Helen. Beside her, Amy cradled Helen's head.

"She's gone," Jana said.

"No," Scott said as he ran to Helen, his heart broken and pain filling his throat and stomach. He suddenly understood the desire to stay on the island and hope the next scenario or dimension might bring back the woman he loved.

"Not Helen. She's okay. We lost Kelly," Jana said, shaking her head.

Helen looked up at Scott as he went to his knees beside her.

Outside, the wind and Utahraptors howled and roared. Time was running out rapidly.

Tom stood over Kelly, and Stu joined him. Neither said anything, but both swallowed hard as they looked at her face, a peaceful, serene face. *At last.* Amy cried hard and hugged Helen, but both looked over at Kelly, confused and sad.

Jered told all of them to get on their feet because they needed to go, but he let Davey lead as they began to move into the other tunnel.

Scott helped Helen, and Jana helped Amy. Stu passed out knives and spears again, and he and Tom fell into place, leaving the cave by the back way.

Mattie watched them silently and didn't move as they left. She had her own plans, which excluded everyone in the group. She would handle things before the creatures got close, and she would pay her dues and pray as she did it.

She thought of RJ, Bobby, Harold, and even Shonna as she prayed. She imagined Air Marshal Lynn smiling at her. As she finished her work, she imagined sitting back in a soft blue plane seat and smiling over at her handsome, smart, sweet son. Mostly, she imagined Jody smiling back at her.

Chapter 26: Redemption

A bird, fleeing the area in fear, caught Jana's hair with his claws but quickly untangled himself and went on. A trio of microraptors ran across the trail and into heavy brush, squealing and hissing with terror as they felt the changing air pressure, rising wind, and an upcoming storm. Dead leaves skittered in the air.

Jana fought another bird, this one bright green-and-orange feathered, but she lost her footing and slid to her knees. One kneecap hit a small pebble, and she winced, sucking air between her teeth. It would bruise badly and make her limp, but she was fine to keep going.

Jered stopped and walked back to help Jana to her feet but froze as a fetid, rotting wind washed over them, something unusual in the fresher breezes of the storm. The stench was disgusting, and he turned his head just as a pair of troodons burst from the bushes.

Disoriented by the storm, nervous and afraid, they had hidden when the humans came along the trail, fearful of a fight. Normally, they would be ready to battle and maybe eat fresh meat, but for now, they were driven by their instincts to go to higher ground. They didn't want to eat or fight or do anything except what their instinct ordered. The woman was in the way.

Like scalded cats, the creatures ran, clawing and biting, trying to get across the trail and find a new one that led farther away inland.

As they ran, they stopped and tangled with the flailing woman and then continued on.

Jered felt ill as he saw that Jana's throat and left eye were ripped and slashed away; the light mist that began to fall made the blood thinner. She barely breathed and made no sounds except a slight wheezing, but there was nothing Jered could do to save her life.

"She's gone," Jered told the others as he caught up and asked, "what's wrong?"

"Helen has some cramps. I'm going to carry her," Scott said.

"Don't let me lose the baby. I wanted to tell you," Helen told Scott.

"You'll be fine," he promised her. He looked at Davey and saw the same fear within his friend's eyes. "Are you with me?"

"All the way," Davey said. Although he knew Helen wasn't very heavy for Scott to carry, he tried to push everyone to hurry.

At the spring, they gulped water, and Helen was no worse. She drank the water and sighed, "Pam was all messed up."

"And Kelly?" asked Scott.

"She didn't say much. We didn't get to talk much. They raped Kelly and Amy. They hurt them, but they planned to eat me," Helen shivered and held Amy close.

Davey stripped off his shirt and buttoned Amy into it so she was covered. She relaxed slightly once she was no longer bare. Helen thanked him. "They saved Pam, and she fell into their gang, I think. She never was very bright, was she?" Helen asked.

"We should've saved Kelly," Stu said, glaring at Tom.

"I had a plan," said Tom.

"And it failed," replied Stu.

"Maybe. Maybe not," said Tom as he looked back at the way they had come and felt like crying. He told them that they only had to run down the trail to get to the beach. They knew this area and could make it on time. What would happen then, Tom didn't know. He didn't want to return but wanted to help the others get rescued.

Scott met Tom's eyes.

Scott continued to carry Helen. As they passed the place that led to the slight clearing where Tom and Stu's father Durango had died from snakebites, Scott shuddered and didn't dare look that way. The bodies would be rotten now, and the bones might be scattered.Their remains couldn't be seen from the trail, but remembering how his friends had died still chilled Scott. Helen moaned as they passed the cut-off trail; she recognized it as well.

Davey stopped and held up his arm. Jered mimicked the motion. Both turned in circles, looking up at the sky. Stu grunted and had a very bad feeling.

"Is the sky getting yellow? I mean isn't a super storm hurricane bad enough without this place playing games?" Davey asked.

"It's resetting. Maybe Kelly…"

"You don't know that. Stop it, Tom. Let her go. Do you think this place really makes us so different? Some say there is always the seed to begin with, but I call it bullshit. There's a propensity for Jody to turn wild and dangerous. Mattie can't fix that," said Scott.

"What's that mean?" Tom asked. They had slowed because they were tired and scared; they talked as they walked.

"I mean we don't devolve that much," Scott explained.

"You sound like Alex," said Davey, meaning it as a compliment.

"Whatever we've become, was always there in the darkest parts of our psyches. Pam was a vain, shallow bitch. I can admit it. I'm not so sure she changed as much as her true nature just came out. Stu is a jackass, but he was always one. Tom, you are paranoid and unsure, and you're full of guilt, but you were always emotional. Davey was always bad assed, but he never knew it until now."

"What about you, Scott?" Davey asked.

"Need for control?" he said, laughed and then sobered. "Kelly was often angry with patients who she said drained the services and couldn't be helped because they gave up anyway. She acted like she wanted to save the world; also, she was very critical. She wanted to decide life and death based on merit. All of you heard her complain about that."

"That's not fair, Scott," Tom muttered.

"Maybe it's true though," Stu said, "and Jody is a psycho, no matter what? You think he can be changed in another scenario?"

Scott shrugged and said, "I don't know. Maybe he can be if he doesn't see his mother die. I just think there was always something wrong deep within. Kelly was the same. We never saw that part."

Stu was quiet as he thought about what Scott said. Stu knew he had always been selfish and had behaved like a tyrant on the island. If he had it to do again, would he make the same choices and be as hard on his own family? He didn't know.

A crash from the beach startled them. The noise was a cacophony of loud bangs. Were huge dinosaurs attacking? Over the roar of the wind, something else did seem to be there. The noise was disorienting. At the tree line, they felt hope. They were almost to their goal. The only problem was that the trees still were undulating, swaying and moving dizzily in the wind.

Scott leaned against one of the trees but jumped right back. The tree was warm and covered in scales, and as he looked, he saw strange colors: variations of aqua to blue green to pale blue to green. He stared upwards, gasped and asked, "What the hell?"

Davey looked with awe and said, "We saw them in the ocean one day and watched them. Benny loved those things, and they sure could swim. He called them titanosaurus. Plant eaters. They love seaweed that grows deep in the water. As they were eating, they dropped some of the seaweed, and Joe gathered it afterwards. It was the best seaweed we had ever eaten...like salted spinach."

The titanosaurus watched the incoming storm a while longer, not afraid of the rising tide, but displeased with the wind and the yellowed sky. He began to move and push trees over by the dozens, trees that were old and enormous yet easily uprooted.

One tree fell across Jered, knocking him down and crushing his ribs and midsection. The titanosaurus stomped his foot on Jered's head, making a sound like a melon bursting.

"Damn," Stu said as he dodged two trees and a dinosaur leg.

As the group ran out from the trees and legs, the titanosaurus turned, thundering to his herd. The bellow was something that sounded like loud, deep tones from a foghorn that would carry for miles even in the wind and drizzly rain.

As asked, the group that they left behind grabbed a few things and went the other way. They were far down the beach where the *Connie Louise* couldn't be swept up and over them, crushing them.

Scott's group came out on the beach where their camp was. It was a mess with everything thrown around and partially covered with seaweed and branches.

Down the opposite way from where their friends had run was a very old sailboat on the rocks; no one moved there either because the entire bottom was ripped out of the old-fashioned boat. Obviously, all the cargo, passengers, and crew had fallen out the bottom on the reefs and gone to the bottom of the white-capped, angry sea.

"About time. We didn't think you'd make it. Because of the storm, the crew had to rush, causing the rescue to be early, so we can't wait," Tyrese had to speak loudly.

"We had a bad time," said Scott.

"Us, too. Dinos and wrecks are washing in everywhere. We've already sent Joe, Joy, Littleton, Benny, Iowa, Michael, and Susan to the ship…well…such as it is. It isn't very much of a ship, to be honest. Skeleton crew."

Scott looked at the lifeboat and snorted. It didn't look very safe to him, but it was all they had. Davey and Trent helped load Helen and Amy into the boat. Davey jumped in as Shannon ordered him to.

Scott blinked away the rain and tried to make sense of the figures, emerging from a jumble of debris and coming toward them on the beach. If the figures were troodons, the group was in deep trouble unless all of them could get into the raft quickly.

"Go, Ty," Scott demanded. Then, he yelled at Stu and Tom who were arguing again. Neither looked around.

"I'm staying to find Kelly," Tom said loudly.

"No, we're going. I'll knock you out and carry you if I have to," Stu responded.

His words were almost drowned out as one of the titanosaurus turned from the tree line and prepared to stalk away. His movements knocked several trees loose, causing them to roll down the beach.

Scott yelled, but Stu and Tom moved far too late. While Stu was spared, one of the huge trees landed on Tom's foot, mashing it into the wet sand. Scott ran to his friend and pulled at the tree, unable to lift it away.

"You have to go. Both of you," Tom gasped. He almost swooned with the pain. "This is no worse really than what I wanted. I want to stay."

"You're crazy," Stu said. He yanked at the tree.

"Now!" Trent screamed from the boat. They were leaving within seconds. Tyrese and he were about to return for the rest, not knowing what was causing the delay. Sheets of rain made visibility poor.

Scott heaved with effort and almost yelped as the shadowy figures began to emerge from the grey mist. Brush and parts of trees blew past Scott.

Then, some of the trash hit them, and Scott went down on the sand, unable to lift his head. He felt as if a truck had hit him. In a dizzied state, he watched a very particular event play out.

"Oh, shit. Unreal," Stu yelled.

"What's going on?" a familiar voice asked.

Scott smiled. One of the shadowy figures spoke and looked like Alex. It felt good to die and see his friend again in his mind. He enjoyed watching the dream-like action. Stu and dream-Alex and the other dream person groaned and tried to lift the tree.

Stu struggled, his shirt bright red. A large branch stuck out of his stomach. Dream-Alex tried mightily, yet he wasn't strong enough, but the third person, the dream person that Scott couldn't quite make out because his face was averted, used all his strength and determination and lifted the tree almost by himself.

Scott dreamed that Davey and Trent lifted him and began to carry him to the lifeboat. In the dream, Davey was excited but also cried in what seemed happiness and sorrow.

"Don't die on me, Scott," Davey said.

"It's okay. I saw Alex again," Scott said. "I'm okay to go. Take care of Helen?" Scott inched toward an inky blackness. He knew he was dying because the hallucinations were so vivid.

In his dream, Scott saw Stu fall back with the branch in his belly, causing blood to soak his clothing. It looked as if Stu gave him a wave and mouthed something about redemption.

Redemption? Was he trying to reset his own fate? Maybe Stu would do better next time, and he'd find Kelly.

Scott figured he'd get to see it all since he was dying, too. His concern was Tom, but there was no need for worry.

As they loaded Scott into the boat, he felt Helen's hands brushing over his arms, but what he heard was the wonderful stuff of dreams and death.

In Scott's dream, he heard someone say something to Tom, indicating that Tom was on the boat and safe. As the darkness began to settle over Scott, he heard a man with a smile in his voice, the man who had lifted the tree from Tom's foot, soothing Tom.

The man said, "I am sorry about Stu, but I am glad to have saved your life. Do not cry, Tom."

Fish.

Again.

Chapter 27: Epilogue

Scott passed out after he heard the dream-voice of a long dead friend. He didn't know how they got from the lifeboat to the small ship that was disappointingly no bigger than the *Connie Louise* had been.

He awoke, a little surprised to be alive, with Helen holding his hand.

The boat rose and sank in the waves, and winds howled as rain battered it. Helen smiled uneasily and told Scott he had been unconscious for only a short time, but that she had been assured he was simply knocked out. He had a lump, his pupils were normal, but he was in no danger of dying.

"I...I had to be. Okay. I hallucinated, I guess. I imagined Alex and Fish appeared and saved Tom and that Fish carried Tom to the lifeboat."

Helen frowned and said, "You didn't hallucinate that. No one knew what was happening, and Tom would have died. Fish and Alex did it. They saved him."

"Impossible. What?" asked Scott.

Helen shrugged and said, "Scott, we know how the island does things, but it isn't the island, is it? It's something that uses storms and leaves things *on* the island. We saw several shipwrecks crash into the island that last hour, and maybe there was a plane, but it was too rainy and too far away to be sure. It was crazy and wild. Somehow, the *Connie Louise* went down again, and Alex and Fish washed up. The time loop was spinning fast."

"Only them?" asked Scott as he felt hot tears fill his eyes.

"Only them. None of the rest, only Alex and Fish washed up right there close to us. Of all places on that huge island, how could that be?"

"God? Luck? Who knows?" asked Scott.

"Exactly, but it happened, and Alex and Fish saw Tom injured and saved his life. They don't remember anything from our scenario. Some of the group told them about the island. I don't know if they believe anything, really, but Fish said it did feel like a nightmare he remembered. He said, 'The story tickles my head. I might recall something as a dream',' repeated Helen.

"Oh," replied Scott.

"Stu didn't make it. Fish said a branch got him."

"I saw that. I don't think he minded much, Helen. He wanted another chance, I think. Maybe with Kelly. I hope she's worth it," Scott said.

"Who knows? In a new loop, she may still hate Stu. I hope...I *really* hope they are good to each other and that it works. If they find each other, I mean. So many variables as Alex or Benny would say."

"They are really Alex and Fish?"

"They really are. Tom lost all the guilt and pain that was in his eyes, and he is over the moon happy," Helen added.

"Happy ending then?" Scott hoped.

Helen chewed her bottom lip and said, "Not exactly. Do you hear the storm? It's bad, just as Susan predicted. Hurricane-type storm, and Scott? The sky is still yellow. Everyone is terrified."

It wasn't enough just to be afraid of a storm that was as bad as a hurricane; it was even worse to be scared because of the damned power used by the storm.

Scott had once thought it might be okay to reset his own scenario, but now that it was a real possibility, he didn't want to wash up on the island again and do things again, like some repeating loop of time. He wanted to be safe with Helen and the baby she was carrying. His baby.

Scott held Helen close and tried to pray, but the choppy seas made it hard to believe anything was okay. The wind increased, and the waves became worse. It was like being back in the *Connie Louise* when a rogue wave picked it up and hurled it across the water, leaving it torn, broken, battered, and ripped open.

Scott wondered if anything had really happened, but instead, he was back on the *Connie Louise*, experiencing that battering again. Maybe he hit his head at that time and had imagined months on a terrible island.

Of course, that was it. He never was on the island of dinosaurs. Alex and Fish never died, or returned. Durango and the others were here with him, and Scott only dreamed of the dinosaurs, snakes, and slugs.

Screaming came from outside his room, and the wood and steel of the small ship squealed and snapped with the pressure of the waves that tried to pull it apart.

When an extra roar filled the room, Scott went flying from the bed and slammed into a wall, and Helen smacked into him. That saved her from serious injury, but the action snapped Scott's arm right above his wrist, making him yelp. His head thumped the wall, and he blacked out.

When he awoke the next time, Helen was beside him, his arm was splinted and wrapped, but he was in vicious pain. However, the sky was blue, and all the violent movements of the ship had ended.

His concern was that instead of a nice, clean hospital room with a television, a pain pump, soft sheets, and fluffy pillows, he was lying on the sand.

"So the *Connie Louise* wrecked, and I dreamed everything?" Scott didn't know if he was relieved or saddened by that.

"What?" asked Helen.

"I dreamed we wrecked on an island of dinosaurs, and much worse, and that there were time loops…Bermuda Triangle crap."

"That was real. We were rescued during another storm. Remember?" asked Helen.

"Oh, why are we…are we wrecked again?" Scott asked.

"We did wreck, but we didn't break up entirely; just the bottom of the ship is gone, caught on the sand. We came to shore as soon as the weather broke. You've got to stop hitting your head."

"Where are we?" Scott asked.

"Somewhere in North America," Helen said.

Scott grinned and said, "We made it home? We did it? Helen, we're home?"

She didn't look pleased but nodded. "This isn't our time, though. The storm screwed up the time for us, like it does to everyone," she said.

"Are we like we were on the island? Back in the days of the dinosaurs? Have we gone back *again*?" asked Scott, feeling tired and dizzy, yet only part was because of his broken arm and his head injury. "But you said we were in North America. How would you know that if we went back in time?"

Helen brushed hair off Scott's forehead and tried to look less depressed than she felt.

It had been difficult during the storms and wreck and then the subsequent evacuation of the boat to explain things to the crew of the ship. Even with Susan there to help tell the story, the events were slippery and hard to grasp long enough to understand.

Helen told Scott that as soon as they washed ashore, they were shocked to see a small pack of compsognathus run by and to hear a big predator roaring from somewhere over the horizon.

"And? Helen, what's wrong?" Scott worried about the lines on her face. Something deep concerned her.

"We're not back in the dinosaurs' time. We're somewhere else in another time or in another dimension, maybe. I guess over a very long time and with many storms, *they* came to us, here. I mean the dinosaurs came to the mainland, the U.S. They came to our time," she said as she raised Scott's head and shoulders so he could sit up.

He almost wished he hadn't seen.

Rows of old buildings, once tourists' shops, dive shops, restaurants, and bars lined the beach. Their colors were long ago faded, the wood was grey and bleached, and many of the buildings were battered and torn apart. Vines grew over broken windows. Telephone and power poles had fallen years before, left to rot in the sand, and not too far from where Scott lay was a rusted shell of a car.

Scott saw a one-armed man, Tom, chase a small raptor away from the car, shouting at it to go away. He felt cheated. "We said we accepted we couldn't come home…"

Helen nodded.

Scott closed his eyes to shut out the reality of what he saw. "There's no home to go back to, is there?"

"All in semantics, Scott. What we have found, is that like it or not, we *are* home."

Over there. I think most of the crew actually survived and they…"

They found dinosaurs, made a fortress, and grew an exceptional garden for their food, Joy explained. She said she thought they did very well, despite the circumstances of the island with all of the dangers. "They lived here, didn't they, Scott?"

"Yes, and I think they lived here a long time. On the other side of the wreck, there is a horrible, pitiful pile of human bones and I think there was a fight with some dinosaurs there on the beach. There are dino bones, but I can't tell them apart except these are big and they had pointed teeth."

"They were here and they died. Some did. Then, a hundred years later, in a storm, they crashed again, but on our end of the island. The ship broke apart and sank and no one survived. Explain that," Harold asked.

Alex closed one eye and warded off a headache. He wanted a drink of the whiskey they brought, but held himself back. "Once they are dead, the ship, boar, or plane can come back again, maybe in a year, or five, or ten. They've gone at least twice, right?"

Scott nodded.

Alex theorized that the *Violet Marie* crashed five years before and all or some died then. He said Littleton, Jada, Benny, and Amy might have died in the crash or lived a while and been killed later. The boat crashed again and those who were dead already, or some of those, were put back in time for a second chance. This time, the four survived the crash.

"Jada told me something strange. She said she had *de je vu*, and felt as if she had been there before and had nightmares about dinosaurs."

"Benny has had them, but Amy said she doesn't and Littleton said he never did, but he said he had a nightmare about drowning," Scott told them. "You're thinking that they have a hidden memory of their deaths?"

www.ingramcontent.com/pod-product-compliance
Lightning Source LLC
Chambersburg PA
CBHW032143170626
46808CB00006B/2344